ME 15.11.13
3 0/6/14

-7 SEP 2021

Return this item by the last date shown.
Items may be renewed by telephone or at
www.eastrenfrewshire.gov.uk/libraries

Barrhead:	0141 577 3518	Mearns:	0141 577 4979
Busby:	0141 577 4971	Neilston:	0141 577 4981
Clarkston:	0141 577 4972	Netherlee:	0141 637 5102
Eaglesham:	0141 577 3932	Thornliebank:	0141 577 4983
Giffnock:	0141 577 4976	Uplawmoor:	01505 850564

Books by Jakob Arjouni

Happy Birthday, Turk! (A Kayankaya mystery)
More Beer (A Kayankaya mystery)
One Man, One Murder (A Kayankaya mystery)
Magic Hoffmann
Kismet (A Kayankaya mystery)
Chez Max
Brother Kemal (A Kayankaya mystery)

BROTHER KEMAL

KEMAL

A KAYANKAYA MYSTERY

JAKOB ARJOUNI
TRANSLATED BY ANTHEA BELL

NO EXIT PRESS

First published in the UK in 2013 by No Exit Press,
an imprint of Oldcastle Books Ltd, PO Box 394,
Harpenden, Herts, AL5 1XJ, UK
noexit.co.uk
@NoExitPress

First published by Diogenes Verlag AG Zurich 2012
Translation from the German by Anthea Bell 2013

GOETHE INSTITUT

The translation of this work was supported by a grant from the
Goethe-Institut which is funded by the German Ministry of Foreign Affairs.
The right of Jakob Arjouni to be identified as the author of this work has been
asserted in accordance with the Copyright, Designs and Patents Act 1988.

A CIP catalogue record for this book is available from the British Library.

ISBN
978-1-84243-965-4 (print)
978-1-84243-966-1 (epub)
978-1-84243-967-8 (kindle)
978-1-84243-309-6 (pdf)

2 4 6 8 10 9 7 5 3 1

Typeset in 11.5 on 13pt Bembo
by Avocet Typeset, Somerton, Somerset

Printed and bound by CPI Group (UK) Ltd, Croydon, CR0 4YY

For more information about Crime Fiction go to crimetime.co.uk/@CrimeTimeUK

For Lucy, Emil and Miranda

Chapter 1

Marieke was sixteen and, in her mother's words, 'very talented, well-read, politically committed, with an inquiring mind and a good sense of humour – simply a wonderful, intelligent young woman, do you understand? Not the sort to hang around idly, not addicted to computers or into nothing but shopping and complaining that life's so boring. On the contrary: class representative, a member of Greenpeace, paints wonderfully well, interested in modern art, plays tennis and piano – or did play tennis and piano anyway...'

Her mother looked briefly at the floor and tucked a strand of blonde hair back from her forehead with her red-polished fingernails.

'Well, that's the way things go, don't they? Right? Two years ago she suddenly developed new interests. I suppose you would say Marieke was what you'd call an early developer. She had her first boyfriend when she was fourteen. Jack or Jeff or something like that, an American, son of a diplomat, in the class above hers. Then at some point it was another boy, and so on. Marieke became something of a live wire, if you know what I mean.'

I knew what she meant. However, not from the photos of

Marieke that I had in my hand. They showed a slightly dark-skinned girl with blonde Rasta braids looking sternly through black-framed designer glasses, with a forced and slightly condescending smile. Pretty, possibly charming, maybe cute if she took off those glasses and looked friendly, but certainly not what you'd call a live wire. More of a short circuit. Leader of a school strike, or singer in a protest band singing songs about animal rights.

What her mother meant applied to herself. *She* was what you'd call a live wire. At second glance. At first glance she was simply one of those athletic solarium blondes with a body that seemed cast out of hard, light brown rubbery plastic: a small pointed nose, full lips slightly too full to be natural, and eyebrows plucked to semicircles as thin as a thread to make her eyes look larger. The eyes were rather narrow, even the plucked eyebrows didn't help that, and anyway it wasn't the size of her eyes that mattered. What made Valerie de Chavannes such a live wire was the blue steel in her eyes, promising all kinds of delights, which she turned on you as outrageously as if she were whispering in your ear: *I only ever think of one thing.* Of course – or at least, most very probably – she didn't have that one thing on her mind that morning; after all, what she wanted was to hire me to find her missing daughter. But at some stage in her life this way of looking at men must have become a habit for her.

When she had opened the door of the villa to me half an hour earlier without introducing herself, I had been more or less sure that she was a visitor: a younger sister who had gone to the dogs, or a pushy tennis-club acquaintance who had just burst in unannounced to deliver the latest changing-room gossip. Along with her I-only-ever-think-of-one-thing look, Valerie de Chavannes wore long, wide-legged, white and very translucent silk trousers that revealed slender legs and a pair of white panties, silver sandals with cork wedges about twenty centimetres high and a yellow T-shirt that was remarkably

10

short and close-fitting for a high society Frankfurt lady and did nothing to conceal her small, firm breasts, leaving so much skin on view right down to the waistband of her trousers that I could see the middle part of a snake tattoo. This was not what I would have expected of a woman called Valerie de Chavannes, daughter of a French banker, married to the internationally successful Dutch painter Edgar Hasselbaink, living in a five-hundred-square-metre villa with a garden and an underground garage in the middle of the diplomatic quarter of Frankfurt.

We were now sitting opposite each other in the sunny living room that occupied nearly all of the ground floor, with white carpeting, modern art on the walls and valuable furniture, with chairs made of leather, chrome and fake fur, sipping green tea from porcelain cups brought to us by a housekeeper of about fifty with a Polish accent. The question urgently occupying my mind was: Did the snake wind its way from her groin up to her navel, or vice versa? And what did it mean, one way or the other?

Instead I asked, 'When exactly did Marieke go missing?'

'At midday on Monday. She was at school in the morning, for a maths lesson, and after that she told her best friend she was going into town to buy a pair of trousers and she'd be back in time for the sports lesson.'

Valerie de Chavannes crossed her legs, and a slender knee pressed through the silk. The platform shoe drew small circles in the air.

'Do you want to tell me the best friend's name?'

'I'd rather... I did say...'

'I know, no fuss, no police, keep it discreet, but I do need some indication who your daughter's hanging out with. Or I'll have to start knocking on the doors of every apartment in Frankfurt, working my way slowly up to Bad Homburg, then through Kassel, Hannover, Berlin, after that maybe Warsaw or Prague – all of them cities for young people eager for new experiences. Okay, not Kassel, obviously.'

She looked at me without a trace of humour in her eyes. The platform shoe had stopped in midair for a moment, and now the circles it drew were larger and faster.

As if speaking to a servant who was slow on the uptake, she explained, 'If everything is all right, and Marieke simply wants to gad about for a couple of days, she'd never forgive me for sending a detective after her. She'd say I was trying to spy on her and interfere with her life. Our relationship isn't entirely easy at the moment. I think that's normal between a mother and a daughter of her age.'

For a Frenchwoman, Valerie de Chavannes spoke German with hardly a trace of an accent. Only now and then did she emphasise the vowels at the end of a word a little too much: *mothaire, daughtaire*.

'Right, then how do you think I ought to begin searching? In the trouser shop?'

Once again the shoe stopped briefly in midair, and Valerie de Chavannes looked at me with barely concealed dislike. All the same, there was still a little of that I-only-ever-think-of-one-thing look left. As if she were turned on by an unshaven, slightly overweight private detective with a Turkish name and an office address in the notorious Gutleutstrasse area who cracked tired old jokes.

Of course it was the other way around: she turned me on, and what I called her I-only-ever-think-of-one-thing look was presumably more an I-can't-believe-I'm-letting-such-a-Turkish-arsehole-sit-here-in-my-elegant-armchair-from-the-Art-Cologne-Fair expression. For some reason she seemed to think she was dependent on me.

'Well... I told you on the phone that Marieke has recently been in touch with an older man – that's to say, older than Marieke, around thirty. He's a photographer, or so he claimed anyway. He said he wanted to take fashion photos of her – the usual chat-up line. His studio or office, or maybe just his apartment, is somewhere in Sachsenhausen. She mentioned Brückenstrasse and Schifferstrasse a couple of times. There's a little tree-lined square. At supper, Marieke talked about a corner café there…'

She cast me an inquiring glance. Did I know the café? The square? Sachsenhausen? Or was Gutleutstrasse all I knew of Frankfurt? Was I exactly what she'd been afraid of finding when she turned to the internet in search of a private detective: a drunken, crude man from a sketchy neighbourhood who had failed at all the professions he'd tried before? Trouble with your ex-wife? Ex-husband? An overdue bill for drugs? Poorly treated by the pizza delivery guy? Kemal Kayankaya, private investigator and personal protection, your man in the outer city centre of Frankfurt!

I sipped the green tea, which tasted like liquid fish skin – or the way that I imagined liquid fish skin would taste – and asked, 'Why did she mention it to you?'

'Mention what?'

'The café.'

For the first time she seemed annoyed. 'What do you mean, why?'

'Well, you say the relationship between you isn't entirely easy at the moment. So why does she tell you about a café where she goes to meet a man who, her mother thinks, is bad company for her? Do you know him yourself?' I gave Valerie de Chavannes a friendly smile.

'I, er, no…' She leaned forward and put her teacup down on the low, cloud-shaped table between us. 'Well, I saw him once by chance when he was bringing Marieke home in his car. We shook hands briefly.'

'What kind of car does he drive?'

'What kind of car…?'

Once again she hesitated. Maybe it was a matter of form, maybe she simply wasn't used to being asked questions by someone she was paying. Or maybe she didn't need a detective at all – at least, not one who found anything out.

'No idea, I don't know much about cars. Something flashy, showy, a jeep or an SUV or whatever they're called, black, tinted windows – maybe it was a BMW. Yes, I think it was a BMW.'

'You did well for someone who doesn't know much about cars. Perhaps you don't know much about number plates either?'

She stopped short, slightly parting her full glossed lips into a moist, narrow slit smile, looking as if I had asked whether I could invite her sometime to a delicious frozen meal and women's all-in-wrestling on TV. I decided to make her stop short like that as often as I could.

Smiling, I raised a hand. 'A little joke, Frau de Chavannes, just a little joke. Tell me what the man looks like, please: size, hair colour and so on.'

This time her hatred of him brought me a prompt answer. 'Medium height, what do I know, neither really short nor particularly tall. Lean build, fit, long curly black hair, in that greasy combed-back style, dark eyes, three-day stubble – good-looking if you like that type.'

'And that type is…?'

'Well, someone looking to pick up girls in a disco, that sort of character.'

'You mean the slimy sort with the carnal stare, heels a little too high and an immigrant background?'

I smiled at her encouragingly.

'If… if that's how you'd describe it…' For a moment she didn't know where to look or what to do with her hands. Then she glanced up and looked at me, sceptical and curious at the same time. 'Just so there's no misunderstanding: no, I don't think so.'

'Of course not. It was only to get things clear: now I know what type you mean. And furthermore, that's why you called me, isn't it?'

'*That's why I called you…?*'

'That's why you called Kayankaya, not Müller or Meier. Because you thought a Kayankaya ought to know how to deal with an immigrant background. What's the man's name?'

She briefly wondered whether to refute what I'd said, and then replied, 'I don't know exactly. Erdem, Evren — Marieke mentioned it only once or twice.'

'You have a certain amount of trouble with the names of your daughter's boyfriends, don't you?'

'Excuse me?'

'Jack or Jeff, Erdem or Evren…'

'What do you mean?' She looked puzzled, then sat up straight in her chair and snapped at me, 'What are you getting at, anyway? Why are you talking to me like that!' All at once she got to her feet and walked quickly to a bookshelf at the other end of the living room. It was roughly fifteen metres away. I noticed her swaying her hips attractively in spite of her rage. From the back, she could easily have passed for a woman in her mid-twenties. With a rounded, taut behind like that, either she spent a lot of time in the gym or Edgar Hasselbaink had struck lucky with her genes.

'I called you to get me my daughter back! I'm just about dead with worry, and you sit here grinning and asking me nonsensical questions!'

She reached into the bookshelf and brought out a packet of cigarettes.

'Well, questions about the name of the man with whom your daughter is presumably involved, what kind of car he drives and where he lives aren't as nonsensical as all that.'

'You know exactly what I mean!' She snapped her lighter, held the flame to her cigarette, inhaled the smoke and angrily blew it out again. 'Have I heard of number plates! Insinuating that I don't remember the names of my daughter's boyfriends! Your manner as a whole…'

She took another drag. 'All that silly sarcasm! And you're

probably just looking at my tits the whole time!' She walked halfway across the room towards me, stopped abruptly and jabbed the fingers holding her cigarette in my direction. 'Either you'll work for me and do as I ask, or I'll look for someone else!'

I let her tantrum blow itself out, watching her breasts, as if she had shown me an interesting detail in the living room furnishings. I thought it was rather funny. She took it sportingly well, shaking her head and laughing dryly as much to express 'I don't believe it!' as 'You've got some nerve!'

'To be honest, I was just taking a look at your snake now and then. At least, I assume it's a snake, but unfortunately the head is out of sight – oh, sorry, I mean the head is out of sight.'

She switched to looking at me as if I were an amiable madman: a friendly, sympathetic and slightly repelled look. She drew on her cigarette. 'You don't say so,' and in her thoughts she was probably running through the list of private detectives in Frankfurt to decide which of them to call next.

'Right.' I put my cup of fish-skin broth down on the glass table and leaned back in my chair. 'So you want me to do as you ask. I'd be happy to do that, Frau de Chavannes, although I'm not sure that you know exactly what you want me to do.'

'Excuse me?'

'Look, this is how I see it, roughly: you met this man – Erdem or Evren – somewhere or other, in the gym, or at a private viewing, something of that nature. He made up to you, and you felt a little curious, maybe along these lines: immigrant background, gold chain, oily hair – you don't meet that kind of person every day, you thought you'd like to hear what he had to say. And when it wasn't just the stupid showing off that you expected – let's suppose he was witty, charming, a little bold, and anyway he could tell stories that you don't often hear at the upper end of Zeppelinallee – anyway, you thought something like: let's invite him to a party, won't Frau von What's-It and Consul Thingummy be surprised! See who Frau de Chavannes has come up with this time! And so all went well, Erdem or Evren was the original party sensation you hoped he'd be, he flirted with Frau von What's-It, he let Consul Thingummy tell him about something of no interest to anyone else, and told crazy stories about his friends, women, cars, the wide world, a touch of the suggestive, a touch of the Oriental, until...'

I stopped for a moment. Nothing of Valerie de Chavannes was moving except the ash falling from her cigarette to the floor, but her eyes rested on me like the eyes of the fish whose skin I had just been drinking.

'...your daughter came home. At her age, parties given by your parents are a good reason to go to bed early for once and conserve your strength for your own parties over the next few days. But then your daughter saw Erdem or Evren, and that was a refreshing change from one of those usually boring occasions with the What's-Its and the Thingummies and Papa's tipsy painter friends – and so on. I may not have the details right, but the general drift of where your problems are coming from must be something of that nature? Of course that's the harmless version. There's another possibility, no party, no husband...'

'Shut up!'

Her cigarette had burnt down to the filter and gone out. All the same, she still held the butt as if she were smoking it.

'I assume that's the reason you don't want me to talk to Marieke's friends? I'd find out that Marieke was going around with one of her mother's acquaintances. Marieke is sixteen, she has a right to do that, and if she's enjoying the situation... she wouldn't be the first daughter in the throes of puberty who wanted to show her mother a thing or two.'

She was looking absentmindedly at the floor. The cigarette end dropped from her hand, but she didn't seem to notice. Suddenly she raised her head and asked, impatiently, 'So now what?'

'So now what?'

'What are you suggesting?' Her voice was harsh and stern, but she was being stern with herself, not me.

'You mean what should you ask me to do?'

'I want you to bring my daughter back!'

'Yes, I know that, Frau de Chavannes. But suppose you were to try Erdem or Evren first...'

'Erden! Erden Abakay. He lives over the café I mentioned on the corner of Schifferstrasse and Brückenstrasse. He's quite well known there, you'd have found him easily.'

'And then?'

'Then you'd have got my daughter out of there!'

'Without telling her I was doing it for you?'

'Of course.'

'And preferably I'd have beaten up Abakay and threatened him – if he ever comes near Marieke again, and so on?'

She didn't reply to that.

'Frau de Chavannes, I'm a private detective, not a bunch of heavies. Once again: suppose you call Abakay first and try to speak to your daughter?'

She shook her head. 'Out of the question.'

'Why?'

'Because I'm afraid of saying something wrong, something to drive her even further into that bastard's arms. At the moment it doesn't take much to make my daughter feel I've said something wrong.'

'Suppose your husband were to call?'

'My husband?' She looked at me as if this were a remarkably idiotic question. 'I definitely don't want to drag him into this.' She turned away and went back to the bookshelf for another cigarette. 'Anyway, he's away. He's guest professor at the Academy of Art in The Hague. He won't be home for another two weeks.' She lit her cigarette, turned to me, and said firmly, 'I want to get this whole thing out of the way by then!'

'Okay, but then please tell me more or less how the story goes. If I come across Abakay I don't want to hear any startling new discoveries. "Frau de Chavannes is my sister's best friend," that kind of thing.'

'Nonsense. It was more or less as you thought. He approached me in the café, and I was a bit curious. A man speaking to a woman alone in a café, where do you find that these days? And I was probably rather bored that morning. We talked, and he was actually amusing – well, amusing in a nightlife, gambling, who-cares-about-tomorrow kind of way. Then he claimed he was a photographer and had taken a series called *Frankfurt in the Shadow of the Banking Towers*. Portraits of low-life crooks, characters, prostitutes, hip-hoppers...'

She cast me a glance. 'I know, not very original, but...'

She was searching for the right words.

I said, 'But together with the nightlife, gambling scene, the who-cares-about-tomorrow attitude, the immigrant background...'

She examined me for a moment as if, once again, she had grave doubts about letting a man like me take a look at her life. Then she drew on her cigarette, blew out the smoke vigorously as if to dispel those doubts, and went on, 'Could be so. I was thinking mainly of my husband.'

'Of course.'

'I knew you were going to say that.'

'What should I have said?'

'Listen: I didn't tell you the truth at first. I hoped to solve the situation just like that. I'm well known in this city, my husband is well known all over the world, while to me at least you are an entirely unknown quantity. And you're a private detective. What do I know about private detectives? If I didn't need help so urgently... Do you understand? Why should I trust you? I'm sure there are tabloids that would pay a few euros for a Hasselbaink mother-and-daughter story about mysterious underground photographers.'

'Maybe there are, but no private detective is going to risk his reputation for a few euros. Our good reputation, so to speak, is our business model – the only one we have.'

While she thought about that, her plucked eyebrows drew closer together, and two small lines appeared on her forehead. I liked the fact that she didn't resort to Botox. Maybe those lips were the genuine article. I'd once kissed a pair of Botoxed lips, and it felt like shaking a prosthetic hand.

She went back to the bookshelf and ground out her cigarette in an ashtray. 'So I can trust you?'

'I won't sell your story to a tabloid, if that's what you mean. Apart from that, I think you rather overestimate the importance of the story.'

'Are you familiar with the art world?'

'I know your husband is a big deal there. Eyeless faces, am I right?'

'That's one of his famous series, yes. *The Blind Men of Babylon.* '

'I've Googled your husband. International prizes and so on. All the same, the kind of tabloids you have in mind don't set out to entertain their readers with people who paint series entitled *The Blind Men of Babylon*. Please tell me what you meant when you said you were thinking mainly of your husband.'

'Will you believe what I tell you from now on?'

'That depends *what* you tell me.' I grinned cheerfully. 'Come on, spit it out. Or would you rather think again about hiring me?'

'I want to...' She hesitated, and for a moment it looked as if she was suppressing tears. She looked at the floor and folded her bare arms, shivering. As she did so the yellow T-shirt moved even further up her taut stomach, and I thought that in spite of the fifteen metres between us, I saw the head of the snake. I'd have liked to know at what point in her life she had decided: Right, now I'm off to the tattoo parlour to have a snake tattooed crawling between my legs. And I'd have loved to know what her parents, Monsieur and Madame de Chavannes, aristocrats from Lyon, thought of it. (I was assuming that you'd be more likely to get a snake tattoo at an age when your parents' opinion still counted for something.) According to Google, since Georges de Chavannes had retired from his position with Magnon & Koch, a private asset management bank, they had been living in a small château in the Loire Valley making their own wine. I wondered whether they sometimes sat over a bottle of it on the terrace looking at the sunset, thinking their own thoughts, and at some point Bernadette de Chavannes asked, in the peaceful atmosphere where the only sounds were twittering birds, chirping crickets and clinking glasses, 'Do you think Valerie still has that terrible...?'

'Oh, please, *chérie*! Let's enjoy the evening.'

And what did Edgar Hasselbaink think about the snake? Or had he perhaps designed it himself? How about Marieke? I wondered how it went down in the school playground. Hey, Marieke, I've got a snake down there too. I'd like to introduce him to your Mama's snake!

'My husband has always found Frankfurt horrible: boring, provincial, uncultivated. Sausages, stocks and shares, brash young bankers, and according to Edgar the locals' favourite drink is a laxative. We came here from Paris ten years ago. By then living in Paris was too expensive for us, and anyway we wanted to go somewhere with fewer exhaust fumes and more greenery for Marieke's sake. Then my parents offered us this house. My father was head of the Frankfurt branch of Magnon & Koch for more than twenty years. When he retired my parents wanted to go back to France.'

'Forgive me, but if you sell the house you can live almost anywhere in the world with the money you'd get for it.'

'When I said my parents offered me the house, I didn't

21

mean they gave it to me. In fact we pay rent, although it's a relatively low rate – that mattered to my parents, as a symbol.'

She paused, went over to a grey corduroy-covered sofa about the size of my guest room, and took a white cardigan off the back of it. As she put the cardigan round her shoulders, she said, 'My parents and I haven't always got on well together.'

'Did you grow up in this house?'

'Yes. I was seven when my parents moved to Frankfurt, and I lived here until I was sixteen. Anyway: we thought it was only for an interim period until we'd decided where we wanted to live. But then... my husband's pictures stopped selling so well, and at the same time we got used to the comfort and size of the house, Marieke was making Frankfurt her home, and so on – many reasons, some of them good, why we're still here. However, my husband has never changed his opinion of Frankfurt and particularly this part of it. You see, he grew up in Amsterdam, he's lived in New York, Barcelona, Paris – in the shabby districts of those cities, I wouldn't want you to think he's missing a life of glamour. When he was studying medicine in Amsterdam, he lived in a student hostel, later often in unheated attics, and in Paris we had a four-roomed basement apartment in Belleville. What he misses here is life with all its surprises. The only surprise you may get in the streets of Frankfurt is when one of the ladies in fur coats walking her permed dogs greets you in a friendly tone of voice.'

Valerie de Chavannes sat back in the Art Cologne armchair opposite me, and I wondered how many fur coats she had hanging in her own wardrobe. Or did the fact that she paid her parents rent mean that no financial support at all came her way from the château on the Loire? But who paid for the housekeeper, the deluxe furniture, the sparkling clean racing bike in the hall?

'So you tried to bring a little of the life he missed into this place in the person of Abakay?'

'He wasn't the first. Whenever I meet someone who I think might interest Edgar, I bring that person home. Do you understand? I do so wish that Frankfurt could be more fun for Edgar. And I thought, well, at least Abakay isn't just sausages and stocks and shares. So I invited him to supper, and it all went terribly wrong. Edgar thought he was a puffed-up windbag, and Marieke took Abakay's side in a pointless discussion about the freedom of art. Only to annoy us, of course...'

Suddenly something unpleasant seemed to occur to her. Or rather, something that was unseemly in the circumstances; something to do with me. For a moment, she looked at me as if she had just that moment noticed that I looked like some bastard out of her past – a teacher with bad breath who felt her up while giving her extra tutoring, or an ex-boyfriend who'd made off with her jewellery, something along those lines.

She lowered her eyes and began massaging her hands. 'Now you know what I meant when I said I was thinking mainly of my husband.'

'Hmm. A discussion about the freedom of art? What was that about?'

She hesitated, looked up briefly, then back at her hands again. She massaged them calmly and regularly. She was good at putting on a show of calm regularity, sometimes of anger and contempt as well. It was only now and then that the mask slipped – and behind it, or so it seemed to me, Valerie de Chavannes was shaking with fear.

'About those stupid caricatures.'

I guessed what she meant, but I said, 'I've no idea what you're talking about.'

'Well, the caricatures of Muhammad. All the fuss about them back then – how long ago is it? Three or four years? You must have heard about it.'

This time she was looking straight at me, and her expression was somewhere between worry and discontent. Was she treading on the toes of a guy called Kemal Kayankaya, or was the private detective, who in the course of this conversation had finally seemed to her like a reasonably civilised person, just an uneducated idiot after all?

'I understand. Yes, I heard about all that. What attitude did Abakay adopt?'

'Well... it wasn't so much about himself – Abakay is certainly not particularly devout – it was about respect for religions in general. Some relation of his, an uncle I think, is an imam in a Frankfurt mosque.'

'Is Marieke susceptible to that sort of stuff?' I looked on the glass-topped table at the photographs of the stern-faced girl.

'You mean religion?'

I nodded. 'Maybe she's not gone off with Abakay after all but with the Lord God Almighty?'

'Oh no, she...' Valerie de Chavannes shook her head, looked despairingly at the ceiling of the room, where her glance lingered briefly as if it showed her pictures of the disastrous evening. 'It was just because of us, or maybe just because of my husband. You see, we're modern, enlightened people, religion has never been important to us or Marieke. And that evening, well, she simply sensed she could make her father go ballistic. If the subject comes up Edgar is an outspoken atheist. He hates any form of religion. And then his daughter suddenly starts defending the veil as a cultural inheritance, an Oriental fashion accessory, a way for a woman to protect herself from men's eyes, and I don't know what else. Even Abakay contradicted her – he could have been privately smiling to himself, I don't know. As I said, it was all pointless. Edgar loves Marieke more than anything, and at the moment she's trying to shake off that love.' Valerie de Chavannes paused, and it was obvious that she was wondering whether to tell me something in confidence. 'You said just now that I didn't seem to know the names of my daughter's friends very well, and by comparison with Edgar you're certainly right. He can probably list the first names and surnames of all Marieke's friends from primary school on. Do you have any children?'

The question came as a surprise, and I thought of Deborah two days ago as we had our aperitif (a term introduced by Deborah; I'd have stuck with, 'I drink a couple of beers before supper') bringing up for the first time her desire to have children.

'No.'

'Love for your children can sometimes become almost monstrous. I hope you realise how important it is for Edgar never on any account to find out that Marieke has been with Abakay. He'd never forgive her.'

'Don't you mean he'd never forgive you?'

Valerie de Chavannes stared straight at me. Her mouth slowly closed, and that I-only-ever-think-of-one-thing expression came back. In fact it was simply a way of looking down on men who, she supposed, only ever thought of one thing when they looked at her.

After a pause, she said, 'You'd have liked it to be a bit more usual, a bit shabbier, right? Or can't you imagine that a woman like me – snake tattoo and so on – doesn't jump into bed with every half-attractive man? Go ahead, as far as I'm concerned – but if you think I'd be idiotic enough to then invite the man to my house for supper I take that as a real insult. Incidentally, in case you're interested, my husband and I are happily married.'

'I'm glad to hear it, Frau de Chavannes.' I nodded to her with my head bent, the way I suppose servants anxious to keep their jobs used to do. 'Particularly for your husband's sake. And I can easily understand that you do not jump straight into bed with every half-attractive man. However, what I don't entirely understand is that with a wife like you – snake tattoo and so on – there isn't something in the air when a young curly-haired underground photographer turns up for supper at your invitation. At least so far as the photographer's concerned, and I'd bet that one or another thought went through your husband's mind.'

'You don't know my husband. He's not the jealous type.'

'In my experience, that's only ever what other people say. And the only man I know who said it about himself became addicted to pills after his girlfriend cheated on him with one of his colleagues.'

'Well, maybe your job doesn't allow you much experience with people whose approach to life doesn't conform to the usual standards.'

'Could be, Frau de Chavannes. But I've met a few fathers who flew off the handle because their adolescent daughters started going around with other men. Among people whose approach to life does conform to the usual standards, that kind of thing is called jealousy.'

We looked into each other's eyes for a moment, and maybe she wanted to hit me.

Finally she looked away and said, 'Right, fine, Herr Kayankaya, obviously you're very articulate, and that's just as well. But it's not really relevant at the moment. Will you get Marieke out of this without letting her know who asked you to do it?'

'I'll try. As I said, your daughter has a right to hang out with Abakay. I can't simply carry her off.'

'But you strike me as a man with imagination. Think up some kind of pretext. Lure Abakay out of town or...'

'Beat him up, yes, I know. But that won't get us anywhere, Frau de Chavannes. And thanks for the bit about the man with imagination. Pay me a day's fee in advance, and I'll see what I can do.'

I took one of my standard contracts out of my jacket

pocket and handed it to her across the glass-topped table. Four hundred euros a day plus expenses, two days' fee as a bonus for success. Normally my daily fee was two hundred and fifty euros a day, but normally my clients don't live in Zeppelinallee. In fact I wasn't all that bothered about the money. I'd had plenty of work recently, and Deborah's wine bar was doing well and becoming a must-visit place in Frankfurt. But as with most relatively cultivated rich people – and I had automatically put the daughter of a French banker and vintner and wife of a highly regarded Dutch artist into that category – it was like this: they pleased themselves and others by supposing that special quality called for a special price, that you had to consider value for money rather than the price itself, that price plus wear and tear of cheap stuff ultimately costs you more than expensive stuff, and so on. It wouldn't even occur to someone with that much money that such an attitude is itself cheap, because attitudes don't cost anything. At any rate, I didn't want to stir up any more doubts in Valerie de Chavannes's mind as to whether she was putting herself into the right hands now that she had swallowed my office address in Gutleutstrasse. I was all the more surprised when she looked up from the document, frowning, and said, 'Four hundred euros a day? Your website said fee by arrangement.'

'If a case seems particularly difficult. In your case I'll stick to my usual conditions.'

'Four hundred euros a day – good heavens.'

She really did seem to be concerned about the amount. It made me feel uncomfortable. On the other hand… I took a look around the living room.

'Do the *furnishings* belong to your parents as well?'

'Most of them, yes.'

It brought me up short. 'And the paintings?'

They were almost all large-format, modern-looking arrangements of blocks of colour, oil on canvas, in heavy, gilded, antique-style frames. Sometimes cubes of assorted colours, sometimes blobs or stripes, a rainbow of merging colours, a red square in a yellow square in a green square, and so on, a purple blotch like a storm cloud. When I looked more closely for the first time, I realised that they could hardly be by the artist who had painted *The Blind Men of Babylon*.

'Edgar would tell you that those aren't paintings, they're interior decoration.'

'Pretty.'

'Exactly.'

We looked at each other, and no one had to say so, but it was clear that her parents were forcing her and her artist husband to leave the pictures hanging on the walls. Maybe they came from the same firm that had furnished the waiting room, the conference room and the lavatory of the Frankfurt branch of Magnon & Koch. Perhaps her parents wanted to tell their son-in-law, as if shouting it through a megaphone, what kind of paintings did not 'stop selling so well at some point in time'. Or perhaps they just wanted to inflict a little torture on their tattooed daughter who had left home at sixteen.

So Valerie de Chavannes was living in furnished accommodation, and four hundred euros was not just chicken feed to her.

'As I assume that I can do the job in a day or so without too much expense, I can offer to halve the bonus for success.'

'Thank you,' she said, and it came from the heart.

She signed the contract, and while she went out to fetch the four hundred euros I put my jacket on and went over to an A4-sized drawing that was fixed to the wall with a drawing pin between two large paintings, a two-by-two-metres rainbow and a three-metres-long row of red and green horizontal stripes. A quick, smudged pencil sketch showing a man with an Afro hairstyle and his mouth wide open, kneeling on the floor between two huge pictures of a

rainbow and some horizontal stripes with a mound of vomit
that reached to his chest and threatened to smother him.

When Valerie de Chavannes came back she saw me
standing in front of the picture.

'This one is funny,' I said, and I meant it.

'No,' she replied, 'it isn't. Here you are.' She came towards
me and gave me four hundred-euro notes. 'I'll be at home all
day. Please call me as soon as you have any news about
Marieke.'

At her daughter's name the strength suddenly drained out
of her. She was breathing heavily, her chin began to quiver
and she pressed her lips together.

'Please bring me my daughter back! And forget about
halving the bonus, that's so stupid, it was only…' She fought
off her tears. 'We really don't have a lot of money right now,
and it was only out of a horrible habit that I thought of it, of
course I'll pay anything you like, just get Marieke back for
me.'

She came a step closer to me, wringing her hands in front
of her stomach and looking pleadingly at me. It was just about
impossible not to put my arms round her. Her head fell on
my shoulder, she gave way to tears and her trembling body
pressed close to mine. She had taken off the cardigan when
she went to find the money, and I was holding her bare
muscular arms. The sleeves of her T-shirt slipped up, and my
fingertips touched her damp armpits. When I began to feel
her breasts through my lightweight corduroy jacket, it was
time to leave.

I carefully pushed her away from me. Her face was wet
with tears.

'Don't worry, Frau de Chavannes. I'll find Marieke for
you. That's a promise.'

She looked at me despairingly. 'If he does anything to
her…'

'He won't.' The things we say. I pointed to the glass-topped table with the photographs. 'Your daughter is a strong, self-confident young woman. And girls her age do gad about. I'm sure the two of them are doing nothing but sitting in a café and talking about underground photography or our anti-social society. Maybe they'll go into the park and smoke a bit of weed now and then. She'll be back this evening, and you can lecture her about the extremely proper things you did at sixteen. I assume there'll be a lot about skipping ropes, poetry albums and classical piano music…'

She had to smile a little.

'See you this evening, Frau de Chavannes. And no, don't stay at home. Go for a walk, or shopping, or to the gym – move about, do something to take your mind off it. But don't forget to take your mobile. I'll call you, okay?'

She nodded, sniffing, and then she said, 'So that's your picture of me, is it? Shopping and the gym, hmm?'

I looked at her for a moment. 'Don't worry about how I see you. Everything is fine there.'

We shook hands, and the next moment I was in the hall. I wiped the sweat from my brow with my sleeve.

The gentleman's racing bike that must have cost five or six thousand euros was leaning against the wall. I'd come to know a few things about bikes since I gave up smoking four years ago. Every time I felt a craving for nicotine that I could hardly withstand I got on my bike and fought the just-half-a-cigarette devil by riding uphill and downhill between Bad Soden and Bad Nauheim, whatever the time of day or night.

Perhaps the racing bike came from financially better times. Or it was one of the things that were meant to give Edgar Hasselbaink the idea that Frankfurt could be fun, and the family scrimped and saved to afford it. Or Valerie de Chavannes, a credit to her financial wizard of a father, had put on a performance for me aiming, just on principle, to lower costs in any situation, however inappropriate.

Just before I reached the hefty, iron-clad front door, a

forbidding sight from both outside and inside, the housekeeper came up the cellar steps with a basket of laundry under her arm.

She stopped in surprise. 'You're still here?'

'Yes. Thanks for the tea. Next time I'd like to try your fish soup, on the reverse principle...'

She gave me a puzzled look.

'Just one question: how long have you been working for the de Chavannes family?'

She didn't like my asking, and if I was not much mistaken she didn't like me either.

'Over twenty years. Why?'

'Only wondering, sheer curiosity. Goodbye, then. Have a nice day.'

She murmured something that I couldn't make out. Was she going to report my visit to Georges and Bernadette de Chavannes? *There was another of them here today...*

When the door latched behind me, I stood in the front garden for a moment breathing in the clear autumn air. Apart from an elderly couple slowly approaching down the pavement, Zeppelinallee was deserted. Not a car driving along, no noisy children, no clinking of crockery, no lawn mowers. You heard the sounds of the city very quietly, as if from far away, although you were almost in its centre.

Both the man and the woman wore Hunter green felt hats, the woman had a fur round her neck, the man carried a walking stick with a gleaming golden knob shaped like an animal's head. The *click-clack* of the walking stick sounded through the silence of the diplomatic quarter.

Let's try it, I thought, and waved to the couple, smiling. 'Good morning!'

As they went on they looked at me as if I were a talking tree or something, and as if talking trees and indeed anything like them were extremely crude.

I took my bicycle, pushed it out of the front garden and

rode away in the direction of the Bockenheimer Landstrasse. As I passed the elderly couple I called out, 'You poorly educated pigs!' And once again they looked, without moving a muscle. A talking tree on a bicycle – what on earth is the world coming to?

I pushed down on the pedals, with the mild October sun in my face, convinced that I had an easy, pleasant job ahead of me. At least, so long as I kept my distance from my client. Valerie de Chavannes was an attractive woman, no denying it, and if I was not much mistaken she wouldn't turn down a little comforting if it was offered in the right way. But there were plenty of attractive women around. I was living with one of them. And anyway, Valerie de Chavannes's I-only-ever-think-of-one-thing look struck me as coinciding exactly with the range of possible feelings about her – and who wanted the hell bit at my age? I was in my early fifties, I did my work, I paid my bills, I had made my way. I'd managed to stop smoking, all I drank was two or three beers in the evening or my share of a couple of bottles of wine with friends, and Deborah and I were planning our future. This morning I had stepped out of my front door generally pleased with life, and I had mounted my bike with an apple in my hand. Not quite heaven, maybe, but not so far from it.

And then I went and did it all the same. I held the fingertips that had just touched Valerie de Chavannes's armpits close to my nose, and caught a faintly lavender-scented smell of sweat, and for a moment I felt as if the October sun were burning down on my head like its sister in August.

Chapter 2

My office was on the second floor of a run-down sixties apartment building – or perhaps it had never run very far up – at the beginning of Gutleutstrasse near Frankfurt Central Station. Pinkish brown plaster was crumbling away from the façade, the bare brick wall showed through in many places, a number of windows had sheets hung over them, others had furniture blocking them, chains of Christmas lights winked on and off all year round on the third floor and on the fourth floor a *Frankfurt Hooligan* decal covered one pane. On the ground floor there was a second-hand clothes shop where you could buy used moon boots, polyester shirts and cracked leather belts. My friend Slibulsky called it the Third Armpit, on account of the smell that wafted out of the shop when the door was open. The front door at the entrance to the building had once been ribbed glass, until a drunk kicked it in three years ago and the owner had replaced the glass with a wooden board.

The stairwell, which was painted greyish yellow, smelled of cats and cleaning fluid. If you found the half-broken-off light switch and pressed it, a candle-shaped naked energy-saving bulb gave just enough dim light to show you the stairs. Some joker kept smearing some kind of sticky substance on the banisters: jam, honey, UHU glue. I was sure the perpetrator was the twelve-year-old son of a single father on the fourth floor, but I couldn't prove it. I once cornered him on the subject, and his answer had been, 'Something sticky? Are you sure it was on the bannisters? Did you wash your hands first?' Little bastard.

A Croatian Mafia, trying to keep me from investigating their shady business, had blown up my previous office thirteen years before. The two-room apartment in Gutleutstrasse had been a quick, cheap, and – I thought at the time – temporary substitute. My fears that, with such an address, and the state of the building, the only clients I'd get would be people with a list of previous convictions or bad drug problems proved to be exaggerated. It's true that with the passing trade that made its way up the gloomy stairs to the second floor merely because of the nameplate saying *Kemal Kayankaya – Investigations and Personal Protection,* I could hardly have earned the rent in those first years. But I had a pretty good reputation as a detective in the city, the word-of-mouth publicity worked well, and business was good. My wish for a classier office space faded. I got used to the area, the chestnut tree outside the window and the little Café Rosig on the corner, until the success of the internet and computer technology made the location of my office superfluous. My clients got in touch by email or phone, my paper files would fit into a shoe box and I held business meetings in the Café Rosig. I could have given my private apartment as my business address. But then Deborah found an apartment in the West End district of the city – four rooms, kitchen and bathroom – and asked if I'd like to move in with her. We'd been at first an occasional, then more and more of an established, couple for more than six years, and I was happy to accept the offer. That meant I needed an office away from my home. If anyone else had designs on me with explosives or anything else, I didn't want Deborah to be affected.

Since my website had gone online, exactly two people had come to Gutleutstrasse unannounced: a woman neighbour who wanted me to get her brother to confess over an inheritance dispute – 'He's a cowardly, soft little worm, you'd only have to squeeze him a bit', and a sad man who had fallen for an anonymous girl in a porn film and wanted me to find her for him. When I explained how much such a search could cost him, and how high my advance was, he went away even sadder than before.

So on the morning when I came back from Valerie de Chavannes's house to my office, I hardly took any notice of the woman leaning against a sunny bit of the wall, talking busily on an iPhone. She wore a blue, expensive-looking trouser suit, and had a short, modern hairstyle. In front of her stood a large leather handbag crammed with papers. An estate agent, I thought. There were constant rumours that the building was being sold to make way for another hotel or parking garage near the station.

I had just put my key into the front door lock and was about to shoulder my bike when I heard her calling behind me. 'Excuse me…! Herr Kayankaya…?'

I lowered the bike and turned round. 'Yes?'

She came towards me smiling, on high heels and with her full and obviously heavy handbag in one hand and her iPhone in the other. She had a broad, friendly face, and the closer she came the more clear it became how tall she was. She was almost a head taller than me; she'd still be half that extra height without her shoes on, and I'm not a short man. I liked to see such a tall woman wearing high heels – she obviously wasn't setting out to do the short people of the world any favours. She let her bag drop to the ground, threw the iPhone into it and held out her hand to me. Her hand was large, too.

'Katja Lipschitz, chief press officer of Maier Verlag.'

'Kemal Kayankaya, but you know that already.'

'I know you from a photo on the internet, that's how I recognised you. The man who saved Gregory...'

She was smiling again, perhaps a little too professionally, and there was a look of speculation behind the smile. Did the name Gregory shake me? Gregory's real name was Gregor Dachstein, and years ago he had won a *Big Brother* TV show, followed by a CD of songs like 'Here comes Santa with his prick, chasing every pretty chick' and 'She's an old Cu-Cu-Custard Pie Baker.' Since then he'd played the clubs in the discothèque world between Little You-Know-Who and Nether Whatsit. Gregory's manager had hired me as his bodyguard for an appearance at the Hell discothèque in Dietzenbach, and the outcome was that I had to take Gregory to Accident and Emergency in Offenbach at four in the morning with about thirty vodka Red Bulls inside him. A yellow press reporter was waiting there with a camera, and for some time after I asked myself whether the manager had arranged with the reporter to be there before the concert, and had organised his protégé's consumption of Red Bull accordingly, or whether the idea of offering a tabloid an exclusive story had occurred to him only when Gregory collapsed onstage. Anyway, two days later a photograph of me with Gregory and my jacket covered with his vomit was published, with a caption saying: *Poison attack? Gregory in the arms of his bodyguard on the way to hospital.* It was an appearance I could have done without.

I responded to Katja Lipschitz's professional smile by asking, 'Would you like an autograph?'

'Later, maybe – as your signature to a contract. As to the reason for my visit to you here...' – she cast a brief, disparaging look round the place: backyard, wood-boarded entrance, all the traffic on Gutleutstrasse – 'would you like to hear it outside?'

'That depends. Does Maier Verlag sell magazine

subscriptions door-to-door? Your trouser suit doesn't look as if a door-to-door salesman could afford it, but maybe that's just because it suits you so well...'

She was brought up short, apparently baffled at least momentarily by the term *door-to-door salesman*. Perhaps she was a neighbour of Deborah and me; you didn't meet door-to-door salesmen in the elegant West End. By way of contrast, three shabby, pale-faced guys had been haunting Gutleutstrasse in the last year alone: 'Want a great deal? *Gala, Bunte, Wochenecho*? Lots of good reading there. Or hey, just give me ten euros anyway, I haven't eaten for days.' It's easier for a camel to go through the eye of a needle than for a poor bastard to scrounge the few euros he needs to survive from a rich man.

She shook her head and said, amused, 'No, no, don't worry. We're a highly regarded literary publishing house. Haven't you ever heard of us? Mercedes García is on our list, and so are Hans Peter Stullberg, Renzo Kochmeister, and Daniela Mita...'

She was looking at me so expectantly that the possibility of my being unacquainted with her authors would have marked me out as a total idiot.

I knew the sixty-something Stullberg from newspaper interviews in which he called for young people to devote themselves to the old values. Reading his words, I thought how writers like to express themselves in metaphors: he was the old values, and the young person devoted to him wore close-fitting jeans and had nicely curved breasts. I'd once seen photos of Daniela Mita in Deborah's *Brigitte* magazine, and it could be that the idea of the young person turning to old values had occurred to Stullberg at the sight of his colleague on the Maier Verlag list. I hadn't read anything by either of them.

'Sorry, of the two of us my wife is the one who reads books,' I said, and couldn't suppress a grin when I saw Katja Lipschitz's slightly forced smile.

I looked at her with a twinkle in my eye and nodded towards the entrance to the building. 'Come on up and I'll make coffee. While I'm doing that you can look through my annotated edition of Proust.'

A quarter of an hour later Katja Lipschitz, now relaxed, was sitting in my wine-red velvet armchair stretching her long legs, sipping coffee and looking round her. There wasn't much to see: an empty desk with only a laptop on it, a bookshelf full of reference works on criminal law, full and empty wine bottles, and a plastic Zinedine Zidane Tipp-Kick figurine from a table football game that Slibulsky had given me. Several watercolours painted by Deborah's niece Hanna, who was now fourteen, hung on the walls, along with a large station clock with my little armoury hidden behind it. Two pistols, handcuffs, knock-out drops, pepper spray.

'Do you have children?' asked Katja Lipschitz, pointing to the watercolours.

'A niece.' I sat down with her in the other red-velvet guest armchair. The chairs were left over from Deborah's past. She had worked for a couple of years at Mister Happy, a small, chic brothel on the banks of the Main run on fair lines by a former tart. When Deborah stopped working there ten years ago, she had been given the chairs as a leaving present.

'Well, what can I do for you?'

Katja Lipschitz looked at me gravely and with a touch of concern. 'My request is in strict confidence. If we don't come to an agreement on it…'

'Anything we discuss will be between us,' I ended the sentence, guessing what was on her mind. 'Forget Gregory. I'm not bothered about him. Gregory's career is over; his manager just wanted to attract attention by hiring a bodyguard. They took me for a ride with that photo.'

'I see.' The words *took me for a ride* were obviously going through her head. The character I want to hire for a delicate job was *taken for a ride* by a third-class (at most) manager and a roughly twenty-second-class beer hall porno pop singer...

'I had no idea who Gregory was,' I said, trying to dispel her doubts. 'The agreement came by fax, and it seemed like easy money.'

'Right.' She put her cup down, looked at one of Hanna's pictures again and pulled herself together. 'It's about one of our authors. He's Moroccan, and he's written a book that's created quite a stir in the Arab world. He'll be coming to Frankfurt for the Book Fair, and he needs protection.' She paused for a moment. 'He's in serious danger. There have been several assassination threats from various Islamic organisations, and even intellectuals are attacking the book and its author harshly.' She pressed her lips together. 'Our publisher is taking quite a risk himself by bringing it out.'

'What's the book about?'

'It's a novel. It takes place in a police station in a fictional Arab setting, although it's obviously modelled on one of the Maghreb countries. Well...' Katja Lipschitz looked me in the eyes, as if hoping to read something there. Her look reminded me slightly of Valerie de Chavannes before she told me that the quarrel in which Abakay and Marieke got involved that evening had been about the caricatures of Muhammad.

I nodded encouragingly. 'Yes?'

'Well, during an investigation in the red light district the central character, a police detective, discovers that he has homosexual tendencies. He falls in love with a boy and they begin an affair, endangering his marriage and his job, in the end even his life. At the same time, of course, the book is really studying the relationship between Muslim society and homosexuality. There are passages in which the police detective – until then a devout Muslim – thinks about the Koran, God and love between people of the same sex, and in his despair and anger turns against his religion. Meanwhile the book also describes an abyss of drugs, sex, poverty and criminality – fundamentally afar from sacred society. Religion is only there to conceal the widespread misery and keep the people calm – do you understand?'

'I do. And the author himself has' – I couldn't resist a slight imitation of Katja Lipschitz's excessively cautious tone of voice – 'homosexual inclinations?'

'No, no, the story is pure fiction.'

'How do you know?'

With the slightly exhausted look that comes into all women's eyes when they are talking about crude, unwelcome advances from men, she said, 'He was at our offices last year, and I accompanied him to several interviews.'

'How big is he?'

'As an author?'

'No, as a man.'

She frowned. 'Why do you want to know that?'

'Well, none of the Moroccans I've met so far are giants, and I imagine that if a rather small man tries making up to such an imposing figure as you I can draw some conclusions about his character.'

'So?' For a moment she obviously thought I was round the bend. 'In fact he is rather small. What conclusion do you draw from that?' Her tone was stern, even a bit angry. Perhaps she didn't like that 'imposing figure', although I had meant it as a compliment.

'If he was seriously interested in you and outward features like size hardly mattered – none at all. But if he is the kind of man who simply tries to jump on anything female, never mind what his chances, from the perspective of twenty-four-hour personal protection that is not a completely irrelevant factor.'

She thought about it for a moment and then nodded. 'Yes, of course you're right. Hmm...'

Once again she thought it over. She disliked the subject, but not as much as she probably should have, given her position. She couldn't hide a certain satisfaction in having to make her views clear because the situation demanded it.

'He certainly doesn't miss out on anything. Or rather, he'd like to think he doesn't. His advances aren't very successful. I spent two days travelling around with him, and he got nowhere with any of the women he made up to. Don't misunderstand me: he's good company, well educated, even good–looking, but...'

She stopped.

I said, 'But he gets on your nerves.'

'Maybe you could put it that way, yes. However, I'm sorry for him. You see, I think he simply doesn't understand that it's different between the sexes here, that communication is more along the lines of equal rights, that we...'

She stopped. The little word *we* echoed soundlessly in the air, as if Katja Lipschitz had farted and was hoping I'd put the sound down to the chair creaking. We, the civilised Europeans Lipschitz and Kayankaya, and he, the Moroccan Freddie the Flirt? Or more likely you two Orientals and I, the tall blonde...?

I tried to help her out. 'You don't have to explain your author to me. I'd just like to know what he does and can or can't do. The reasons don't matter to me.'

'I just didn't want you thinking that he...'

'Pesters women?'

'Well... no... yes, I definitely didn't want that.'

'Don't worry. Besides, he'll leave me in peace. What languages does he speak?'

'Hmm...' She wanted to say something else about her author, but then let it rest. 'Arabic, of course, French and German. He studied in Berlin, and always spends several months a year there. And incidentally... he chose you.'

'He chose me?'

'Well, we showed him a list of all the Frankfurt agencies offering personal protection, and he thought it would help his

41

public image if his bodyguard was a Muslim. You are Muslim, aren't you?'

'Oh, well.' I gestured vaguely. 'My parents were. I mean my birth parents. They died early on, and I was adopted by a German couple who raised me. I assume they were baptised, but religion didn't play any part in our family.'

Katja Lipschitz hesitated.

'But... forgive me for asking, presuming we're to work together it might not be totally unimportant: how do you see yourself? I mean are you religious in any way?'

I shook my head. 'No religion, no star sign, no belief in hot stones or lucky numbers. When I need something to lean on I have a beer.'

'Oh.' She looked confused and slightly repelled.

'I'm sorry, I can't offer you any faith. But that can hardly be of any importance to the public image of your author. My name is Kayankaya, and I look the way I look. I don't know how Muslim I am under religious law, but ask any of my neighbours, I'm sure they could tell you.'

'Do you mind if I pass that on to our author?'

'Not in the least. So he chose me. Was it his idea to hire a bodyguard in the first place? Does the information that his book is causing an uproar in the Arab world come first and foremost from him?'

Katja Lipschitz's glance lingered on my eyes for a moment. But she wasn't seeing my eyes, rather something or other beyond them – her boss, a furious Freddie the Flirt, or the newspaper headline: Moroccan author invents role of victim to crank up sales of book.

'That's nonsense,' she said at last, but she didn't sound entirely convinced.

'Glad to hear it. I've been rather suspicious ever since Gregory, as I'm sure you'll understand. What's your author's name? Well, I can find that out anyway: Maier Verlag, Morocco, gay police detective – Google ought to provide enough hits. And then I can convince myself of the outrage in the Arab world.'

'Malik Rashid. I'll be happy to show you the threatening letters.'

'In Arabic?'

'We'll get them translated, of course. In case we're forced to publish them, or we have to turn to the police.'

'If you hire me I really would like to see those letters.'

I looked at the time; it was just after noon. I'd determined to get Marieke home in time for lunch. On the one hand, the fastest possible performance of a job is of course part of the service; on the other hand, I liked the idea of impressing Valerie de Chavannes with my swift, uncomplicated help.

'When does the Book Fair begin?'

'Next Wednesday. Malik is arriving on Friday and staying until Monday.'

'Is he staying at a hotel?'

'The Harmonia in Niederrad.'

'Not a very cheerful neighbourhood.'

'We're glad to get any hotel rooms at all. You may not know it, but Frankfurt is fully booked during the Fair.'

'I'm only wondering what Rashid's evenings look like. People don't usually like going home to Niederrad early.'

'He has engagements on all three evenings – dinner with the publisher, a reading and a panel discussion, and after those he'll be exhausted and want to go to bed.'

'Does he drink alcohol?'

'He says not, for religious reasons, but to be honest... well, I've seen him at least once when his conduct made me think he was under the influence.'

'Maybe he smokes weed?'

'I... you'll have to ask him that yourself. You see, I've tried to avoid personal subjects between us as much as possible because...'

'Yes, I understand.' I nodded to her. 'Fine, Frau Lipschitz, I have enough information for now. I assume you'll want to think it over. You can call me anytime.' I took one of my business cards out of my shirt pocket and gave it to her. 'My usual fee as a bodyguard is a hundred euros an hour plus taxes, but for round-the-clock standby duty, at least a thousand euros a day, plus taxes. If Rashid gets drunk or catches flu and spends all day in bed it will still cost you just under a thousand two hundred euros. However, I'm flexible about calculating working hours: for instance, if Rashid wants to go to the cinema or something like that, and I can go for a coffee in the meantime, I won't sit outside the cinema and claim I was searching the street for Al-Qaeda for two hours on end.'

'I'll have to discuss it with the publisher.'

'Do that. And if we come to an agreement, please let me know as soon as possible so that I can check out the hotel before Rashid arrives.'

She nodded. 'And in that case I would also send you his daily schedules.'

'Great. And the threatening letters.'

'And the threatening letters.'

'I'll wait for your call.'

We rose from the armchairs and shook hands. Then I showed her to the door and out into the stairwell, and pressed the light switch. The energy-saving bulb shed its cool grey light.

'So what *is* the title of Rashid's novel?'

'*Journey to the End of Days.*'

'Ah. Does something like that sell well?'

'The advance orders were enormous. With a subject like that... and although the book is only just out, everyone's already talking about it. That's why we're so anxious in case anything happens during the Fair.'

We nodded to each other once more, exchanging friendly smiles, and then Katja Lipschitz made her way downstairs. I thought of warning her about the low ceiling on the last landing, but then let it be. She must have enough experience with low ceilings to notice, and judging by her reaction to my remark about her imposing figure she would rather do without further references to her size.

Back in my office, I typed, 'Malik Rashid: *Journey to the End of Days*' into the Google search box. Among other links, I found the Maier Verlag website. The novel had appeared in Paris a year before, and the French critics quoted by the publishing house were of course over the moon about it. Even elsewhere on the internet I found, almost exclusively, praise for the book. Apart from a comment in a blog from one Hammid, who hated it like poison. Or at least my tourist French was enough for me to get the drift of *un roman de merde* and *sale pédé*. But as far as I could tell there were no reactions at all from Morocco or any other Arab country. So the fact that, according to Katja Lipschitz, the novel had caused a great stir there was a pure publicity spin. That was fine by me. Easy money again.

I took the station clock off its hook, opened the safe behind it and put the pistol and the handcuffs in my pockets. They should at least make a bit of an impression on Abakay if necessary. Then I shouldered my bike and set off for Sachsenhausen.

Chapter 3

The sun was shining on the terrace of the Café Klaudia,
where people were sitting eating lunch or a late breakfast.
Talk, laughter and the clink of crockery mingled to make an
inviting cloud of sound. I padlocked my bike to a traffic sign
and went to the front door of the building, which was next
to the terrace. There was a smell of raw onions, and full glasses
of cider shone golden and enticing on the tables. 'The locals'
favourite drink is a laxative, Edgar would say.' That had even
annoyed me a little when Valerie de Chavannes shared it.
What was the damn Dutchman thinking of?

The front door of the building was not locked. I found
Abakay's name on the list beside the doorbells, went into the
hall and climbed the stairs to the third floor as quietly as I
could. But it was an old building, and the wooden steps
creaked. When I reached the second floor, I thought I heard
another creak from above me.

I didn't exactly know what I was planning to do. Listen at
the door, ring the bell? 'Good morning, Kayankaya here, city
gasworks, you must have an old pipe in there somewhere
that's been supplied with gas by accident, may I take a quick
look through the rooms?' Or, 'Hey, Abakay, old boy!

Remember that night at the club the other day? You gave me your address, and here I am. It's me, Ali!' Or simply, 'Hand over the girl or I'll smash your face in!' And suppose no one came to the door? Did I wait on the stairs or in Café Klaudia? Or stroll around and keep my eyes open for the pair of them?

I didn't have to know for certain. I didn't have to know at all. On the third floor the door to Abakay's apartment was open. On the floor on the other side of it, a fat, half-naked white man was lying on his back. He wore jeans and white sports socks, and his paunch bulged over the waistband of his jeans like a large flatbread dough. His head had fallen to one side, his face was turned to me, saliva was running out of his mouth and his eyes had a blind, staring look.

I took my pistol out of my jacket pocket and got close enough to him to see what was wrong: a small stab wound to the heart with blood seeping from it. Next moment I heard a door close, and someone in the apartment called, 'Okay, I've got the stuff, we'll be ready soon.' And after a short pause: 'Herr Rönnthaler?'

Another pause, and then footsteps approached. I got behind the doorframe, took the safety catch off my pistol, and peered into the front hall of the apartment. Abakay – shoulder-length hair, black, gleaming ringlets, little moustache as narrow as a pencil stroke, a white shirt unbuttoned to the waist, black waistcoat from a suit, thick gold rings on his fingers – bent over the body.

'Rönnthaler...?!'

I had no time to think about it. When Abakay raised his head and looked around I walked into the apartment, pistol pointed at him.

'Damn it, what the...?'

'Where's the girl?'

'What?'

'Tell me where she is or you're next.'

He put his hands up in a placatory gesture. 'Hey, man, I've no idea what's going on here!'

'The girl!' I was fingering the trigger.

'Yes, yes, it's all good! She's in the room over there! Everything's okay! Please don't...'

I hit him hard over the head with the pistol, his knees gave way, and he sank to the floor beside the other man's body. I spent a moment listening for sounds in the stairwell. I'd thought I heard a step creaking again, but all was quiet. I took Abakay by the arm, dragged him over to a radiator and handcuffed him to the pipe. After that I quietly closed the door and quickly walked through the apartment.

A long corridor, a lavatory, the living room where the TV set was on but muted, an open bottle of Aperol, an empty bottle of prosecco and three half-full glasses. Opposite the living room was a very tidy, spotlessly clean kitchen with a second door into the apartment between the china cupboard and the dishwasher. It was not shut, and it led to the back stairs. On the kitchen table lay a plastic bag containing five little balls of silver foil. I opened one of them and touched the white powder inside it with the tip of my tongue. I wrapped up the ball of silver foil again and hid the bag of heroin in a drawer under a stack of frying pans.

The next room was furnished as an office: a desk with a computer and printer, a bookshelf full of coffee table books and several cameras, on the wall a large, framed black-and-white photo of a good-looking young couple drinking coffee in Paris, with the Eiffel Tower in the background. Abakay, the good old underground photographer!

Next was a bathroom, with marble tiles, also spotlessly clean, and the corridor with more framed black-and-white photos to the right and left – trees, girls, cats, cloud formations – and finally a door with the key in the lock. I bent down to the keyhole and tried to see past the key and listen for sounds. It was an old door with a hefty lock, and there was a gap a millimetre wide round the key. All I could see through it was a white wall, and I couldn't hear anything. On the other hand I could smell something. Something disgusting. All of a sudden I was panic-stricken. I imagined Marieke lying on the floor after an overdose, choked by her own vomit. I turned the key and pushed the door open.

At first I was dazzled by the sun shining in through the window. Then I saw Marieke. She was sitting naked on a king-size bed covered with gleaming white satin sheets, leaning against the pillows with her arms round her knees and holding her legs close to her body, and covered from head to toe with vomit. Grated carrots, bits of tomato, half pieces of pasta. Because the window was closed, the sour smell rising from the bed was overpowering.

Although she was obviously shaking with fright, she gave me a nasty, challenging, sick grin.

'Another one?! I don't believe it! Well, come on then! I've tidied myself up a bit for you. I hope the vomit doesn't bother you. Want to lick it off me? Does that turn you on?'

Her stomach was rising and falling fast, like a dog's. The harsh, faraway look in her eyes said: I'll kill you if there's any way I can do it.

'Listen, I'm not —'

'Here, have some pasta!'

'I don't want to do anything to you. I've come to get you out of here.'

'Oh yes? And drag me off where, you bastard?'

I shook my head. 'I'm from the police. Paolo Magelli, special plainclothes unit. We've been after Abakay for some time. I'm sorry we came on the scene so late. Do you have any injuries?'

Her glance was still hard, and she didn't take her eyes off me for a second, but gradually the madness disappeared from them, making way for distrust. Her folded arms dropped, barely perceptibly, and the tension left her body.

'Show me your ID.'

'I'm sorry, we had to move fast and I left my jacket in the car. I'll show you my ID when we're down there.'

'We're going down to the street?'

'Of course. I'll take you home to your parents or wherever you live.'

'Where's Erden?'

'Lying in the front hall. Unconscious. We had to knock him out.'

'And that fat bastard?'

'Beside him.'

Marieke stared at me for some time, then unfolded her arms and began massaging her hands, which were probably numb with tension, and looked down at herself.

'I'd like a glass of water. My throat is sore after all that throwing up.'

'Did they give you drugs of any kind, or…'

'No, no, I stuck my finger down my throat. I thought that might turn him off.'

'Wait a minute.'

I went into the kitchen and ran a glass of tap water. I listened for a moment, in case Marieke was taking her chance to run for it. But when I went back she was still sitting on the bed, now with the bedspread wrapped round her body. Only then did I notice that her lips were swollen.

She drank the whole glass, and said, 'Thank you.'

'Would you like to shower before we leave?'

Once again distrust flickered briefly in her eyes. Was this just a trick? Did I simply want her clean and smelling nice before I attacked her?

'We can go like this if you'd rather. I just thought… well, so that maybe you can forget a bit of what happened here.'

'I won't forget it.'

'Of course not…' I hesitated. 'May I ask you a few quick questions?'

She looked at me expressionlessly and then looked away at the window. 'Okay, and then, yes, I would like to shower after all.'

'That's fine.' I went to the window to open it and let in some fresh air. When I reached for the catch, Marieke said, 'Forget it.'

The window was specially made: soundproof armoured glass, mirror glass on the outside, with a safety lock. I shook the catch in vain.

'Why do you think they could leave me alone here?'

I tried to ignore the stench.

'First, could you tell me your name?'

'Marieke de Chavannes.'

'How long were you shut up here, Frau de Chavannes?'

'Since just now when that fat bastard attacked me.'

'Judging by your swollen lips you defended yourself.'

'I did.'

'And then?'

'Then Erden was suddenly totally normal again, and he said he'd get something to relax us. After that they locked me in.'

'When did you realise what they were planning to do to you?'

She looked away and pulled the bedspread more tightly around her shoulders. After a while she said, 'When that fat bastard leered at me in such a funny way. I tried to run for it. I still thought he was just trying it on, do you see? Between old buddies. That was how Erden introduced him: "Meet my old friend Volker, he wants to get to know you." So I thought I could just get away quickly, I even went to get my bag.' She shook her head. 'And then the fat bastard was after me – incredible!'

'Was there anyone in this apartment but you, Erden and the fat man?'

'No. Why?'

'Just a routine question.'

'What's happened to the fat man?'

'Something's the matter with his heart. My colleagues are just ringing for an ambulance.'

'Hopefully he croaks!'

'Hmm. And Erden?'

'What do you mean, "and Erden"?'

'Do you hope he croaks, too?'

She hesitated, opened her mouth and looked inquiringly at me, until her thoughts seemed to go elsewhere, and her eyes still lingered on me as if by chance.

'I don't know. He's so...' She stopped, and cautiously felt her lips with her fingertips. 'Until just now we were still friends.' For a moment she looked as if she might burst into tears, but then she just sighed sadly. 'We had fun, I don't know how else to put it.'

'Hmm-hmm.'

Her glance was sharp again. 'Not the way you think. You see, Erden's a photographer. That was what mattered most to both of us. Art. He takes wonderful photos, photos with a political message. One series is called: *Frankfurt in the Shadow of the Bank Towers*. Portraits of desperate, sad faces, but so beautiful. And there were other pictures of Frankfurt...' She hesitated, and then added, with a precocious air: 'The city of little men in suits and roast beef sandwiches.'

'Did Erden say that?'

'No, my father.'

'What else did you talk about?'

'Oh, how should I know? All sorts of things: music, hip-hop, our origins, what our parents do, what films we like. For instance – and now that I think of it I can't make it out – we went to see *The English Patient* together, and he said it was one of his favourite films. Do you know it?'

I knew about ten minutes of the film, and after that I'd gone to sleep on the sofa beside Deborah. 'I don't think so.'

'It's such a romantic love story! Imagine – and then this!'

'You said you were friends until now.'

She hesitated, suspicion in her eyes.

'Yes?'

'Were you a couple?'

There was a pause. She looked at the sheet in front of her. After a while she said, 'I'd like to shower now.'

'Okay, then I'll leave you alone. You know where everything is. Meanwhile I'll go and see how my colleagues are getting on with the fat man and Abakay.'

She looked up. 'I don't want to see him now.'

'Of course not. Don't worry, my colleagues have probably taken him away.' I nodded to her. 'Call me when you're finished.'

She watched me head to the door.

'Tell me...'

I turned. 'Yes?'

'Will my parents hear about this?'

I shook my head. 'I don't think you'll be needed as a witness. Nothing really happened to you – forgive me for putting it like that, but I have to say so from the legal point of view – and there'll be plenty of other women to give evidence.'

'You mean there were other girls before me?' she asked, and I had the disagreeable impression that she'd have liked to be the only one.

'Frau de Chavannes, in case this isn't clear to you yet: Abakay is a pimp. And if girls didn't want to go along with him he pumped them full of heroin. You can forget about art and romantic films. You happened to be lucky.'

And with that little lecture I left her alone. Abakay, Abakay, I thought on my way along the corridor, you really have a knack for it: a little social kitsch, cheap drinks, terrible films, and great big gold rings on your fingers, and the girls come running! I wondered whether Valerie de Chavannes herself had landed in those white satin sheets after a couple of glasses of Aperol.

When I reached the front hall of the apartment Abakay's mouth was open, he was groaning, and he was clearly about to come back to his senses. I hit him on the head again with the pistol, and then I searched his pockets. In his trouser pocket I found one thousand two hundred euros in hundred and two-hundred-euro notes, along with some fives and tens. Presumably there had been exactly one thousand five hundred there an hour ago. Maybe Abakay had made out that Marieke was a virgin; that would have explained the high price. Then Marieke had been difficult, and to calm her down Abakay had gone to buy heroin with some of the money he had obtained in advance from fat Volker. One thousand two hundred and a few squashed notes were left.

I took the bigger bills and stuffed them into the pocket of fat Volker's jeans.

Then I went into the kitchen and searched the drawers for a sharp knife. The shower was running in the background. I hoped Marieke would never tell her mother that she had slept with Abakay.

I returned to the entrance hall of the apartment with a butcher's knife about thirty centimetres long, knelt down beside Abakay, and cut and stabbed him lightly in the chest and the stomach. Not deep wounds; I just wanted it to look as if there had been a fight, and I wanted Abakay's blood on the blade. Abakay groaned again and twitched, but he didn't come round. I crawled over to fat Volker, wiped the handle of the knife on my T-shirt, and closed his cold hand round it. The small wound, level with his heart, had stopped bleeding.

I took a roll of parcel tape from the office, a teacloth from the kitchen, gagged Abakay and bound his legs together.

After that I went back into the office, turned on the computer, and typed 'Marieke' into the window of the search engine. The name appeared on a list of various girls' names with pseudonyms after them. The pseudonym Laetitia, in brackets, followed Marieke's name, and then it came up in a kind of catalogue. The file was entitled 'Autumn Flowers 2011'. The photographs were simple snapshots of fully clothed teenagers in the street or cafés, usually laughing. Laetitia was described as: *Clever, demanding upper-class girl, political interests, likes conversations, will go to great lengths in her search for adventure if the tone is right, ready for almost anything, exotic, milk-coffee colour, very well developed, still fourteen for several months.*

Fourteen; that accounted for the price.

Another girl with the pseudonym of Melanie was described as: *Happy, natural suburban girl, loves horses, likes to have fun – laughter above all. More for the conventional ride than delicate games, blonde, fresh, youthful type. Sixteen.*

Probably eighteen.

And then there was Lilly: *Super special! Sweet little mouse in knee-length socks, still plays with dolls, virgin, to highest bidder.*

I deleted all the data about Marieke, typed *de Chavannes* into the search engine, brought up Valerie de Chavannes's address and a few photos of her taken secretly in the café. I deleted those as well. In the bookshelf I found a carton of photographs labelled *Frankfurt in the Shadow of the Bank Towers*. With the carton under my arm I went into the front hall and kicked Abakay as hard as I could between the legs. In spite of the gag he grunted out loud, fluid ran from his nose, and he doubled up before falling on his side unconscious again.

'That's from Lilly.'

As I waited in the kitchen for Marieke, I leafed through the photographs. Most of them were black-and-white photographs of devastated, wrinkled, old or prematurely aged faces against the background of the high-rise bank buildings of Frankfurt. An old Roma woman with a toothless grin and a cigarette end in the corner of her mouth, a dark-skinned youth with an Elvis quiff, a child's guitar and only one eye, a junkie whore with an entirely vacant expression and an *I Love Frankfurt* button on her blouse, and so on. Not so bad, but not so new either. I felt as if I'd seen these photos many times before.

I put the carton aside and wondered what weapon, or what tool, could make such a narrow but deadly wound.

Chapter 4

We reached the inner courtyard by way of the back stairs, and went through the gateway to the street. The aroma of grilled meat wafted out of the kitchen windows of Café Klaudia. It was lunchtime, and I felt hungry.

'We must find a taxi. My colleagues used our car to take Abakay away.'

'How about Volker?'

'There's a doctor with him in the stairwell.'

'Why didn't you want us to go out the front?'

'So that he wouldn't see you again. There are cases where the customer, or rapist or whatever you like to call someone buying underage girls for sex – anyway, there are cases where the man tries making advances to his victim later, especially when it went wrong the first time. Naturally we want to avoid that. I don't want him to get a chance to imprint your face on his mind.'

'I don't think he's feeling very well.'

'He'll soon be better.'

We were standing on the pavement, and I was looking out for a taxi. My bike was gleaming in the sun twenty metres away.

'Won't he have to go to prison?'

'What for?'

I looked at her. After her shower, the blonde Rasta braids tied behind her head with a blue velvet bow, in jeans and a white blouse, the square-framed designer glasses on her nose, she looked just like the stern and slightly condescending girl in the photos on Valerie de Chavannes's glass-topped table. She'd been in shock half an hour ago, but it was clearly wearing off.

'Attempted rape?'

'It's always rather difficult to prove that kind of thing. Particularly when the alleged victim has previously had a voluntary relationship with the pimp involved.'

Marieke's features froze. For a moment she looked as if she were about to turn and march away, maybe spitting at my feet first, or something like that.

'You're wrong!'

'Am I?'

'Erden isn't a pimp, he's a photographer, and what's more he's a good friend of my mother!'

'No, *you're* wrong there. Maybe he's a friend of your mother, but if so he's not a good one.'

She shook her head in annoyance.

'Erden's far from being a pimp! He just wanted to do Volker a favour, he needed money and Volker has plenty of it. And to be honest, if he hadn't behaved like such a pig with that nasty talk, and wanting me to get undressed at once and so on... I'm not usually such a prude.'

She gave me a brief, inquiring look, to see if I was shocked, and then went on, 'And that's why there weren't any other girls before me. You just thought that idea up to make it all worse. Because you're a policeman and so that you can put Erden in a cell. Maybe you'll get a pay raise or a medal or something!'

'My God! If people got medals for arresting little bastards like Abakay, I'd have gone into the metal trade long ago.'

'Very funny.'

'Apart from that – well, I don't know how you imagine a pimp, but pimps with any intelligence at all will of course go to great pains *not* to resemble the image of their profession.' As I said that, the big gold rings on Abakay's fingers flashed into my mind, and I thought that either he was less intelligent than I had assumed, or I had less of a grasp of the subject than I thought. Maybe pimps with any intelligence at all played about with the familiar notions because that sort of thing turned some women on. The way Deborah had first turned me on in a bar at three in the morning: high heels, a generous décolletage and an eloquent smile, speaking in an affectionate whisper – 'You're something special. I can see that right away, and I'm something special too – together, darling, we'll fly through paradise all night, only four hundred marks.'

'That doesn't make Abakay's profession other than what it is... It's like petrol stations that advertise their concern for clean air.'

Marieke did not reply. She was staring furiously ahead, both hands clutching the straps of her leather bag, presumably deep in thought about my coarse and heartless nature. Compared to Abakay: cuddles, sweet talk, sensitive films, sympathy, artistic talent, social responsibility – why had she freaked out like that when he said: 'Darling, I'm sure ours is a great love, we're so lucky, but to live with that great love we need money, sad to say those are the facts of society, so be nice to Volker, he's a good friend who needs a little affection, and snogging a stranger can't affect our great love, can it?'

Maybe we ought to have left through the front door after all, I thought. Volker's corpse and the gagged body of Abakay would presumably have been impressive enough to keep Marieke away from the apartment for some time.

'How are your lips?'

She kept her eyes on the ground.

'I expect Abakay might not have hit you so hard but for those rings...'

'Stop it! It was a scuffle! Don't you understand? An accident! And we were all a bit drunk.'

'If you carry on in that vein you'll end up in court as a witness after all, but for the defence.'

'Do you know what he needed the money for?'

'No idea. Golden ornaments for his prick?'

'You're just disgusting! For a Roma family in Praunheim. He wants to film a photo-documentary about their daily life. Dreadfully poor people, no social support, not even health insurance, nothing at all, with five children – and people are always complaining about beggars, but what else can they do? And do you know the worst of it? The grandparents were murdered in a concentration camp. This is Germany! I know what I'm talking about... My family's relatively prosperous, but look at the colour of my skin, my father is black, so for the people around here I'm like a Gypsy, a foreigner! And that's what Erden wants to achieve with his photo-documentaries: he wants all the foreigners, people of other colours, from other places, of other faiths, all the outcasts to get together and form a movement and later a political party. The Foreigners' Party! Wouldn't that be wonderful? I mean you're an Italian or something. Magelli, wasn't that it?'

'What's the name of this family?'

'What?'

'The name of the Roma family in Praunheim. A family with five kids and no medical insurance – well, of course that won't do. I'll call social services and make sure they get insurance as quickly as possible.'

There was a pause, and Marieke stared at me, taken aback.

'Is that meant to be another joke? Are you laughing at them?'

'Not in the least. But to help them I'll need their name or their address.'

'I suppose you think they haven't tried everything already?'

'Then some social worker may have committed an indictable offence by refusing them insurance. Medical insurance is obligatory in Germany. In the interests of and for the protection of the community as a whole. Imagine if the children are incubating some dangerous infectious disease and not getting treatment. Or the family is living here illegally – in that case I'd get in touch with an organisation that helps refugees and knows all about such cases.'

Marieke was still looking at me as if I wanted to stamp the Roma family's papers as 'to be deported'.

'Or maybe this family doesn't exist at all? Could it be just a symbol? The Roma family in Praunheim with forebears murdered in a concentration camp, shunned today as they always have been? I can easily imagine that as a photo-novella.'

'Do you know something?' said Marieke, suddenly very calm and determined. 'I really, really don't like you. Now please take me home.'

We spent the next five minutes standing side by side in silence. Marieke was looking straight ahead, deliberately unmoved, while I looked up and down the street in search of a taxi. As I did so, my eyes fell on the blackboard outside Café Klaudia, with the dish of the day written in white chalk: shashlik on a skewer with rice and red peppers.

A shashlik skewer, I thought, would leave a thin, narrow wound behind.

I wanted to ask Marieke to wait a minute so that I could ask the waiter whether there had been a skewer missing when he cleared the plates away in the morning, and if so whether he could remember the guest who had taken it, but just then a taxi came round the corner. I put off questioning the waiter until I came back for my bike, and flagged down the cabby.

'Where do you live?' I asked.

'At the far end of Zeppelinallee,' replied Marieke, looking at me for the first time in five minutes. If I was not much mistaken, there was a touch of triumph in her eyes.

'Well, that's a terrific district. Maybe a little too noisy and exciting, isn't it? It wouldn't do for me.'

She rolled her eyes. I laughed, and held the door of the cab open for her.

Chapter 5

'Marieke!'

Valerie de Chavannes ran through the front garden, swept her daughter into her arms and fell with her to her knees, hugged and kissed her, with tears running down her face.

'Marieke, my darling! My dearest darling!'

'Hello, Mama,' said Marieke. She returned the hug, but apart from that let her mother's greeting wash over her.

I stood at the garden gate, watching the scene and trying to smile like a friendly police officer.

After a while Valerie de Chavannes cast me an inquiring glance over her daughter's shoulder with her happy, reddened eyes.

I tapped my forehead. 'Magelli, Frankfurt Police.'

'Oh.' Valerie de Chavannes acted surprised. 'Police?' she asked, without letting her daughter out of her arms.

'Mama, I…'

'Nothing bad happened,' I said, interrupting Marieke. 'In the course of our investigations into a drug dealer we met your daughter in the apartment of one of the dealer's customers. According to your daughter, he's an acquaintance of hers. As we had to take the customer to the police station with us as a witness, we thought it would be best to bring your daughter home.'

Marieke turned her head to me, looking surprised, and then almost grateful.

Her mother said, 'Drugs?' And to her daughter, whom she was still hugging, 'Darling, you haven't been taking drugs, have you?'

'Oh, Mama, at this moment that's...' Sighing, Marieke broke off what she had been about to say.

I said, 'There are no signs at all that your daughter has been consuming any drugs. She probably went to see her acquaintance about a photo project. *Frankfurt by Night*, something like that.'

Once again Marieke turned her head in my direction, but this time to look at me as if she couldn't quite grasp what a primitive arsehole I was. Frankfurt by night! If the Foreigners' Party was ever really founded, I probably wasn't going to get an invitation from Marieke to become a member.

She freed herself from her mother's arms, got up from the garden path and reached for her leather bag. 'I'm going in now, I'm rather tired. I'll tell you all about it later. Is Papa back?'

'But darling, Papa won't be back until next week.'

'Oh no, so he won't. Did you...' Marieke cast me a quick sideways glance.

'No, I didn't tell him anything.'

'Okay. Then I'll go in.' But she turned to me once more, looked at me and finally said, surprisingly seriously and from the heart, 'Thank you, Herr Magelli. For the taxi, and everything else.'

I nodded. 'You're welcome.'

Valerie de Chavannes and I watched Marieke as she disappeared through the open front door into the hall of the villa. Then Valerie de Chavannes stood up too, brushed the dust off her white silk trousers, and looked anxiously into my eyes.

I raised a hand in a soothing gesture and said softly, 'It's all okay. As far as I can judge, they really were just talking about photographs. As I suspected: a little dream to change the world, a little creativity, a little tea drinking. And as for Abakay' – I lowered my voice a little more – 'I think you'll be rid of him for a time. Probably a very long time.'

Valerie de Chavannes closed her eyes in relief, and ran her hand over her face, rubbing it. 'Oh God! Thank you – thank you very, very much!'

But when she dropped her hand and opened her eyes again, the anxious look was back. 'What do you mean by a very long time?'

'Well, maybe two or three years. I'm not a judge.'

'You mean he'll have to go to prison?' Her voice took on a touch of hysteria – whether for joy, or horror at having come so close to a kind of criminality that could carry a jail sentence, I wasn't sure.

'I'd assume so. But I'd rather not explain the circumstances. If Abakay ever finds a connection between you and me, I think it will be better if you know as little as possible about the dirt he has sticking to him. Let me reassure you: his criminal deeds have nothing to do with Marieke. Abakay is a nasty character, but as for your daughter, I think he tried more or less the same number on her as he did with you: *Frankfurt in the Shadow of the Banking Towers*, social injustice, blah blah blah…'

I was thinking of the trembling girl I had found in Abakay's apartment, smeared with her own vomit, and I wasn't feeling very good about it.

So I didn't immediately notice the change in Valerie de Chavannes's expression. All of a sudden I took in her horrified, injured look. As if I'd insulted her severely. And then I realised why: *as for your daughter, I think he tried more or less the same number on her as he did with you.*

And because *the same number as he did with you* really mattered in only one context, the next question was obvious.

Valerie de Chavannes took a deep breath before saying, with as much self-control as she could manage, 'He didn't pull off any number on me. He'd have liked to, but let me make it clear to you, Herr Kayankaya: it didn't work.' And then, visibly summoning up all her courage, she asked, 'Do you think Marieke has slept with him?'

I hesitated. Her seriousness was infectious. 'I've no idea, but I don't think so. Marieke seems to me too sensible for that. Maybe they made out a bit...'

...Clever, demanding upper-class girl, political interests, likes conversations, will go to great lengths in her search for adventure if the tone is right, ready for almost anything...

'You don't have children, do you? You can't know how much I hope you're right.'

'I can imagine, though.'

'Suppose...' She stopped, thought about what she wanted to say. 'Suppose Abakay doesn't have to go to prison – maybe a clever lawyer could fix it for him – and then he turns up here again?'

Something told me that this question didn't come out of the blue. Valerie de Chavannes had an idea, and it had not occurred to her only this minute.

'I don't think that will happen. And if it does – I can offer you my services. You know my fee.'

She didn't respond to the last remark. 'Why don't you think it will happen? He's seen the villa, so of course he thinks we're exceptionally wealthy. And how often does a man like that come so close to real wealth? He'll try getting whatever he can out of us.'

'Well, yes, but he's done that already. He's made advances to both the ladies of the house, I gave him a bloody nose for one of those occasions, what can he do now? Steal your letterbox, I suppose. I can always get that back if it's worth it to you. But as I said: Abakay will be going to prison, I assure you he will.'

For a moment she looked desperate, as if I were slow on the uptake. Then she glanced quickly at the neighbouring properties to the right and left of the villa, at the open front door behind her and up at the windows – no sign of life anywhere there – took two steps towards me and whispered, 'And suppose he tries blackmailing me? He can do that from prison, or get some friend of his to do it.'

'Blackmail you? Hmm…' I scratched my throat with one finger and asked, in as neutral a tone as possible, 'But what could he blackmail you with?'

'How do I know? He'll simply think something up. There's always something that could be used.'

'Well, there aren't a thousand possibilities. Either you've committed some kind of crime – cheated the taxman on a grand scale, something like that, and you're being pestered about it with emails, recorded phone calls –'

'Or as I said,' she interrupted me, 'he'll think something up. Something that could conceivably be true and ruin my reputation – that sort of thing's been known to happen.'

'Hmm. For instance, that he had an affair with you?'

'For instance. And then I'll have to prove it isn't true. It's just crazy!'

'Yes, that would indeed be crazy.'

We looked at each other for a while. Then I said, 'And what are you suggesting to me now?'

She swallowed, and a pleading expression came into her eyes – a plea for understanding, help, pity. When she slowly opened her mouth, her lips were trembling. 'You said just now you gave Abakay a bloody nose. Well… I'm wondering how far you would go in that direction…? For payment corresponding to the job, of course. I mean – Abakay is a nasty piece of work, you said so yourself, and I know what a bastard he is…'

I was less surprised than might have been expected. For one thing, it wasn't the first time I'd had such an offer put to

67

me; for another, there'd been something of this nature in the air all along. Valerie de Chavannes wanted Abakay to disappear from the face of the earth.

'Do you know what he said when he was leaving after that supper here, and we were alone in the hall for a moment? He told me I'd never sleep easy again until he had a large slice of my cake. And by *cake*, of course he meant the house and what he thinks I have in the bank. Then, two weeks later, my daughter disappeared. Do you understand? Even if he goes to prison for two or three years – what are two or three years to a man who thinks he has the opportunity of a lifetime? And we are weak people, soft art lovers, people who read books – we don't stand a chance against someone like Abakay. Suppose he goes to The Hague to see my husband tomorrow, tells him lies of some kind, maybe threatens him or even beats him up? My husband would give him anything he asked. Out of fear, and what else could he do? Call the police? Nothing has happened yet. What was it you said this morning? At sixteen Marieke has the right to go out with a man. And don't tell me there are no drugs involved! I don't mean smoking a bit of weed, why would he go to prison for that? So stop telling me fairy tales!'

I looked at the villa to see if there was any activity at the windows. In the last few minutes Valerie de Chavannes's voice had risen louder and louder. But I couldn't see either Marieke or the housekeeper.

Now Valerie de Chavannes wasn't looking at me with pleading in her eyes, but like a wild animal. A mother animal who would defend her young however bloody the fight. And she wanted me to decide: was I for her or against her?

As calmly as possible I said, 'I'm not telling you fairy tales. Abakay won't be going to prison for dealing drugs but – or if I were the public prosecutor this is how I'd construct the case – for murder.'

I emphasised the word *murder* clearly. Presumably there

were several ways of nailing Abakay: for trafficking in minors, pimping, sexual abuse, abduction, rape, drugs — and maybe murder too, depending on how you interpreted the scene in the front hall of his apartment, but that made no difference to me at the moment. I just wanted to utter the word *murder*. Valerie de Chavannes had to hear the precise description of what she was suggesting to me. Never mind *I'm wondering how far you would go in that direction...?*

'It will probably be hard to pin murder on him, but who knows?'

'Murder...?' Obviously my remarks had had the desired effect. Valerie de Chavannes looked as if someone had kicked her hard in the behind.

'That's what it's called when someone is killed, however much of a bastard he is. Incidentally, you get far longer than two or three years in prison for it. And you know something? I wouldn't even like to spend a weekend in there.'

'But... but why would Abakay murder someone?' There was horror in her face.

'As I said, I don't want to explain the circumstances. Try to forget Abakay, be glad you have Marieke back, and above all, never ask anyone again to kill for you. Because from that moment on, if he plays his cards right, well, he has you firmly in his power. And how would it be if it wasn't Abakay but a slimy little private detective from Gutleutstrasse who wanted his share of your cake?'

She was still looking at me in horror, and then increasingly in confusion and embarrassment. In the end she just looked downcast. She turned her eyes away and looked at the flowering shrubs. After a while she said, 'I don't think you're either little or slimy.'

'Thanks, but I didn't mean it literally; it was just making the point.'

'And I'm sorry. I don't think I really expected you to go along with my proposition...'

'That's all right.'

'If it was only me, but Marieke and Edgar…' She went on staring at the shrubs. 'Have you ever been really afraid? I don't mean facing a gun, or fear of flying, or anything like that, but permanent, constant, daily fear?'

I thought it over. 'Once, when it began to dawn on me that I'd made a bad mistake. Perhaps that's the worst fear – when you're afraid you've messed things up yourself. But if I may say something to you; if anything should happen to Marieke or your husband, it's not your fault. You meet characters like Abakay in life – at least, if you ever step outside your front door – and we're none of us fast or experienced enough to get away every time. It's just bad luck.'

'I invited him to supper.'

'Yes, bad luck, and maybe a bit of naïveté, but it has nothing to do with fault. You don't have to make up for anything, understand?'

'Oh, Herr Kayankaya…' She sighed, turned away from the flowering shrubs, and her glance rested heavily on me. 'Do you know something? Right now I really want to hug you.'

'Oh.' I felt slightly dizzy. 'Hmm… But would your daughter understand that if, for instance, she saw us through the bathroom window?'

Her eyes were still on me, feverish, inviting, her breasts rose and fell in time with her breathing, which came shorter now.

I tried to keep the friendly policeman smile going, and offered her my hand. 'Let's leave it at that, Frau de Chavannes. I'll send you my bill within the next few days, and if Abakay happens to make any more difficulties, which I don't expect, then call me. Otherwise: best of luck.'

'Herr Kayankaya…'

She took my hand and pressed it first strongly as if to say goodbye, before she then simply held it in hers, soft and warm, and went on looking at me. The warmth passed into my body and constricted my throat.

At last I withdrew my hand and cleared my throat. 'You're good at that, aren't you?'

She slowly let her arm drop. 'It's nothing to do with being *good* at anything.' And with a slightly dreamy, fragile smile: 'It just happens.'

'I see...' I pulled myself together. 'Well, as I said, the best of luck.' And when she still didn't move: 'Look...' I pointed to the villa. 'Your daughter.'

Valerie de Chavannes spun round in alarm, saw the empty window and the empty front door, turned to me again and looked first surprised, then indignant.

I shrugged my shoulders. 'It could have easily happened. Then you wonder whether you really had to let something happen.' I raised my hand in greeting. 'Have a nice day.' Then I quickly turned away, went through the garden gate and down Zeppelinallee. It was so quiet that one or two minutes later, when I had almost reached the next crossing, I heard the heavy front door of the de Chavannes house latch. I was extremely glad that I'd only given Valerie de Chavannes my hand.

Chapter 6

I sat down in the café on the Bockenheimer Warte, ordered a double espresso and called an acquaintance in the Frankfurt Police.

Octavian Tartarescu, despite his name and his Romanian origin, looked like a typical German country boy. Or, rather, exactly as anyone would imagine a German policeman. Tall, strong, short fair hair, a pronounced, angular chin that looked made for the straps of a helmet to be buckled under it, blue eyes with a serious and rather pitiless expression, his mouth a narrow line suitable for barking out orders, and his cheeks white and plump from eating potatoes every day. Instinctively and without meaning it as a compliment, total strangers called him 'cop' during any bust-up in the streets, even if he was neither in uniform nor driving a police car. It was simply the first term of abuse to occur to anyone looking at Octavian. Nonetheless, his superior officers liked to send him on undercover missions, on the assumption that no criminal would expect the police to be so stupid as to infiltrate the underworld with someone who looked as if Himmler himself had had him bred to maintain public order. Still less did they think that criminals would believe them clever enough to do that very thing.

It was as an undercover cop that I had first come to know him twelve years ago. At the time Deborah was still a prostitute. I had helped her to get rid of her pimp the year before, found her a place in Mister Happy, and since then, so to speak, I'd been her favourite customer. Octavian was tracking down a ring of sex traffickers who smuggled Belarusian girls into Germany. In the role of a slightly simpleminded punter, he was combing the brothels of Frankfurt, and so one evening he came to the small establishment on the banks of the river Main. Mister Happy was probably the last place in Frankfurt's red light district that would have illegal, under-aged, forced sex workers. At the time I'd known Tugba, who ran the place, for years. She was a women's — or more a prostitute's — rights activist. She'd worked as a prostitute herself, and become famous all over the country because she had drawn a pistol and forced her pimp and a hated customer, whom her pimp had repeatedly forced on her, to fuck each other. To emphasise her point she shot both of them in the legs several times and then called the police. The press was full of the case for weeks. Tugba, who came from a Turkish family from Darmstadt, hired a good lawyer and got off with a suspended sentence on the grounds of self-defence. With the help of an investor and the money she had made from interviews and her own TV documentary show — *Horizontal with My Head Held High* — she had bought the old boathouse on the Deutschherrnufer not far from Offenbach. She had it well renovated, uncovered the original timber framing of the façade, furnished bright and friendly rooms with views of the river and put in a sauna, several small fountains with mosaic tiling and a comfortable bar on the ground floor with leather chairs and a silver counter. Over the terrace she stretched wires and planted roses to climb them, and to its left and right she placed two old streetlights specially delivered from Hungary. When the weather was warm enough, the girls could lean against them for the delectation of the customers. A picturesque wooden landing stage went out over the river, with fragrant lilacs and willow trees trailing their branches in the water in spring. The background music from the bar was exclusively piano: Keith Jarrett, Ahmad Jamal, Mendelssohn, Mozart. Tugba was very particular about that. She had a passion for the piano, played the instrument herself and probably had not entirely given up her dream of a career as a concert pianist. All things considered, if the Michelin Guide gave stars to brothels, Mister Happy would have had three of them.

That evening, Octavian saw me sitting on a bench on the landing stage reading the newspaper, and said to himself that no punter would spend his time in a brothel that way. He came down from the terrace, said good evening, asked if he could join me and I thought: This guy looks like a cop.

He asked me this and that as one punter to another, what the place was like, the service, the girls – he really did say *girls*, in English – and I thought: A cop from the countryside – before asking whether I worked in Mister Happy.

'You mean do they provide guys here as well as girls?'

'No, no…' As far as I could see in the evening light, Octavian's potato cheeks went red, and I thought: A gay cop from the countryside – well, best of luck in Frankfurt!

'I heard…' he went on. 'Well, between you and me, I like girls really young, specially Russian chicks, so I thought if you work here, as a manager or for security… see what I mean? Well, I thought maybe you'd know whether there was anything of that nature to be… well, to be had here. It's my first visit to this place.'

Now I did take a closer look at him. He was playing the embarrassed country bumpkin pretty well. Maybe not a policeman after all? But I was no criminal, and I had known a lot of clever policemen.

I put my paper down. 'Show me your badge first, and then we'll see what I can do for you.'

'My badge?'

'Well, or your ID − anything to convince me that my information will end up in the hands of the law and not some wretched little guy who fucks children and is trying to pretend he's an undercover cop.'

'Eh?' Octavian, annoyed, made a face. The country bumpkin act abruptly disappeared. 'What sort of crazy act are you putting on?'

I later learned that he'd had a long day − spent in dirty, stinking brothels full of teeny bopper entertainment and striptease, and had planned just to look in quickly on Mister Happy, which he knew to be a well-run establishment, and then finally have a beer in a place where he wasn't forced to look at bare breasts the whole time. Some smart-ass like me was the last thing he needed.

In a bad temper, he asked, 'Are you one of us, or what is this crap?'

'Kemal Kayankaya, private detective. A friend of mine works here, but I'm not her pimp. No pimps allowed in Mister Happy.'

He hesitated for a moment and then replied, 'Octavian Tartarescu, vice squad. Is there a beer to be had here at anything like a normal price?'

'If I get it for us. Jever, Tegernsee Spezial − or one of those Belgian beers with champagne corks, but they're expensive.'

'Do they play golf here too, by any chance?'

I fetched us two Tegernsee Spezials, and then another two and then four, and so on. It turned into a really good evening. The sun sank into the river Main, the glowing sunset sky was reflected in the mirror-glass of the high-rise façades opposite, water splashed from the fountains around us, slow jazz piano music with a double bass came from the bar, and we talked about Frankfurt and the lives that had brought us here. One of us Romanian, the other Turkish − we fell into a kind of homeland euphoria for the city. The prettiest park, the best restaurants, the best Frankfurter green sauce, the lousiest but funniest beer kiosks, the best tramline for looking out the windows, the best high-rise building and so on, until after a while we came to the best place on the banks of the Main, and after about eight beers each that was, of course, where we were at that moment. Presumably we would have agreed on the Mister Happy landing stage even without the beer, but probably not so exuberantly.

And when a while later we were speaking and fondly mocking the Hessian dialect, both for fun and to prove how at home we were in Frankfurt, the thought briefly crossed my mind that the Turk and the Romanian might not really be as sure that they belonged here as they had thought. At least, I knew no Hans-Jörg from Frankfurt who would have celebrated his city so euphorically and with such childish pride – the city where, since the day he was born, he had never had to struggle with the registration office, hear himself slammed at the regulars table or wince at the slogans of election campaigns.

'Octavian?'

'Kemal. What's it about?' Cool, professional, chop, chop. Even though we hadn't spoken to each other for months. When Octavian didn't have a number of beers under his belt, his manner suited his appearance. That was probably why we were more acquaintances than close friends.

'I've got something for you: pimping, child abuse, rape, drugs, murder...'

'Hold on a minute, I'll get a pen and paper.'

At the word *murder* I thought of Valerie de Chavannes. How had she been planning to pay me for the job? Or had her talk of being short of money been only a tall story to beat down my fee? Or had she thought that a more passionate embrace or a canvas in *The Blind Men of Babylon* series would do the trick? Had she already checked out how much a contract killing would cost?

'Okay, carry on.'

'The pimp and his customer are lying in an apartment in Schifferstrasse in Sachsenhausen. Café Klaudia is on the corner, the apartment is on the third floor above it. The customer is dead, murdered; the pimp is tied up and chained to a radiator.'

'Tied up by you?'

'Yes. His name is Abakay. He trafficks in underage girls; you'll find all the details on his computer. Look for a file called 'Autumn Flowers'. I got one of the girls out of there. She's my client's daughter, and I hope I've deleted all references to her from the computer. She's not available as a witness, but you'll find plenty of other girls.'

'Who's the murderer?'

I hesitated for a moment. 'When I got into the apartment the customer was dead, a narrow stab wound to the heart, and Abakay was standing over him bleeding from the chest. The dead man was still holding a kitchen knife. I assume it was a quarrel about money. Anyway, I didn't find a murder weapon.'

'How about the knife?'

'Too broad. You'll see, it's as if he'd been stabbed with a knitting needle.'

'Are *you* available as a witness?'

'If I don't have to give my client's name.'

Octavian paused – it was a pause that he meant me to notice. Then he said, 'A knitting needle. That's the kind of thing you might expect to be a girl's weapon. I hope you're not shielding a murderess.'

'Nonsense,' I replied, but at the same moment I thought: Interesting. But Marieke could hardly be as cold-blooded as that; hearing me coming upstairs, hurrying into the bedroom, finger down her throat… All the same, I'd have liked to pay a quick visit to Abakay's apartment to look for a needle or a shashlik skewer under the bed, just to be on the safe side.

'Right. Then I'll go straight there.'

'The heroin is in the kitchen under a stack of frying pans.'

'You must have really turned the apartment upside down.'

'That's exactly what I did. See you soon, Octavian. Call me if you have any questions.'

I closed my mobile, drank my espresso and looked at the time. Just after two. It would take the police several hours to search Abakay's apartment, and I didn't want to be seen around there until they were through with it. Although I'd told Octavian I'd be available as a witness I wasn't sure about that. In all probability, Abakay knew people who could make life very uncomfortable for hostile witnesses, and I wasn't up for that sort of thing anymore. In fact, ever since my office was blown up I'd been more cautious in general, and now I was sharing a four-room apartment in the West End with a woman who wanted to have my child. I had a great deal to lose, and that mattered to me more than whether Abakay got two or five years in jail.

That was why I wanted to avoid being seen with Octavian and his officers for now. I could still simply deny playing any part in the case.

I decided to leave questioning the waiter about the shashlik skewer and fetching my bike until the evening. Instead, I went to my office through the West End and the rail station area in the autumn sunlight, got into my new old Opel Astra, and drove to the Brentanobad stadium. There was going to be an under-fifteen girls' football club game there at four o'clock, and Deborah's niece Hanna was playing in defence.

Chapter 7

Deborah's real name was Helga; she had adopted Deborah as a stage name when she was working as a table dancer and prostitute. Deborah was her grandmother's name. When I asked why she had chosen to work as a stripper under the name of a relative who I knew was close and dear to her, Deborah had answered, 'Because I loved her very much and she wouldn't have minded. This way she's always with me, if you see what I mean. I was nineteen when I came to Frankfurt, and life here wasn't always easy, so I needed someone.'

Deborah came from Henningbostel, a village of a thousand inhabitants near Bremen, and at the age of eighteen she had followed a young man called Jörn to Klein Bremstedt, fifteen kilometres from her hometown. Jörn expected to take over his father's pet food factory at some point. After two months in the attic storey of his parents' guest apartment, Deborah knew that she wanted more from life than the smell of pet food and evenings spent watching TV with her future in-laws, and she packed her rucksack. At first she got *less* from life, namely a job at a checkout counter at Aldi five kilometres farther in Jösters. After a while she packed her rucksack again and went on, hitchhiking with the goal to reach a university town. She had no high school diploma so she couldn't hope to study, but she thought a university town would be full of young people and something would turn up. She had considered Bremen, Hamburg or Hannover, but then a couple of teachers and their kids gave her a lift in their motor home from the Oyten service station all the way to Frankfurt; and because on the one hand Deborah expected more of life but on the other she had the modest undemanding north German nature, she was satisfied with her new place of residence, even though she knew nothing about Frankfurt before, except its name. She stayed with the teachers for a while, looking after their two small children, then began working as a waitress, moved into a shared flat and at some point decided to earn enough money to open an espresso and sandwich bar in Henningbostel. She missed her parents, her friends and the flat northern countryside; Frankfurt felt more and more like a huge, cold monster, and espresso – real espresso, not the bitter dishwater that came out of the drinks machines in bars in Jösters or Oyten – was something she got to know and learned to love at Café Wacker on Kornmarkt. In fact she had a natural bent for gastronomy. She found few things in life more fun than eating, and to this day I have found few things in life more fun than watching her at it. She ate like a cow – slowly, with relish, letting nothing disturb her. When she stood at the stove in her wine bar, making bean soup or lamb goulash, you felt she'd like to send the customers away and empty the pan all by herself, with a bottle of cool red wine to go with it.

Her homesickness for Henningbostel wore off over time and Frankfurt became her new home, despite her work in the sex trade. The dream she still cherished of a restaurant of her own helped her through many long and sometimes unpleasant days and nights on the job. In her leisure time she tried out restaurants, went to wine tastings and took cookery courses. We became more and more of a couple, and I was glad when, after a year at Mister Happy, she had got together enough starting capital to leave the sex trade and rent a premises in Bornheim for her bar. Deborah's Natural Wine Bar, serving simple food and light, fresh wines, quickly became successful. Soon she could afford to bring her elder sister Tine, recently divorced, and Tine's daughter, Hanna, from Henningbostel to Frankfurt. Tine was now working as a secretary for an insurance company, and she and her daughter lived in the Hausen district of the city. Hanna often came to see us, did jobs in the wine bar during her school holidays and was probably one of the reasons Deborah wished to have children. Two days ago, when we were drinking our aperitif and Deborah had said, 'Kemal, I want to have a baby,' I flippantly slipped, with her professional past in mind, 'Who with?' Whereupon she had marched off in a furious temper.

But ever since, that remark had kept going through my head, and it was the reason I spent a free afternoon watching two under-fifteen girls' football teams rather clumsily kicking a ball about. I wanted to find out what it was like to stand with other fathers and mothers on the sidelines, a stale beer in my hand, watching kids stumbling over a football.

'Hi, what are you doing here?' asked Hanna when she spotted me after the game among the spectators, some fifteen of us in all. She was a tall, thin girl with a pierced tongue and blond hair irregularly cut with a beard-trimmer to a length of more or less a centimetre. She usually wore boy's clothes, shabby trainers, cargo pants, baggy T-shirts in washed-out colours, and sometimes a scarf twisted thinly round her forehead. When she did that she looked like a jungle guerrilla fighter; I called her Rambo once, and she asked, 'Who's that?' She had a delicate, pale, beautiful face that easily went unnoticed with the look she affected. For a while I thought she might be a lesbian, but of course I didn't mention that to anyone. I could do without Deborah's head-shaking and Tine's indignant, 'Oh, of course, just because a girl plays football!'

But then Hanna had her first boyfriend, a very popular character at her school, laid back, a skateboarder with a Leonardo DiCaprio look, and I saw that a girl who to me resembled an undernourished aid worker with a hair problem was obviously attractive to her own generation and in her own surroundings.

'I was passing by, had some free time and wanted to see how you lot played.' I gave her a thumbs-up. 'Terrific!'

'Oh, come on, don't pretend. Do you have your car here?'

'I do.'

'Can you give me a lift?'

'Sure. Where to?'

'I'm ravenous – would you invite me to a meal?'

'Okay, but in Sachsenhausen. I have to pick up my bike there.'

After she had showered and changed, we drove to Café Klaudia. There was a police car outside the door leading to Abakay's apartment. We sat on the terrace, and Hanna ordered spaghetti with vegetable sauce and an apple–juice spritzer, and I had a cider. Hanna told me about the other girls on the team, their coach, her school, her plans to go on holiday with Leonardo DiCaprio, and I realised that we were attracting looks from the neighbouring tables – ah, Papa with his lively daughter! – that were not unwelcome to me. Genetics would have had to be in an unusually experimental mood to link my features with such a blonde, fair-skinned outcome as Hanna. However, we obviously gave off such a strong father-daughter aura that our very different outward appearance didn't matter to those around us. Then I tried imagining that Hanna really was my daughter: a few of my genes, a few of my little habits, maybe a similar way of walking or smiling, her hair dyed and not a genuine blonde, and an Asiatic brownish complexion behind her fashionably pale makeup. But it didn't work. I still saw Deborah's sister's daughter sitting there, and although I was fond of her I felt no impulse to take her hand with its bitten fingernails or to invite her to the cinema or anything like that. All the same: for the first time I was curious what such a feeling would be like.

When the waiter brought the bill, I asked if he happened to have noticed a shashlik skewer missing when he was clearing tables sometime shortly before noon.

'Happens all the time – people are always going off with cutlery or cups or whatever else,' replied the waiter, a young man with pearl earrings, a mop of frizzy hair and a dragon tattooed on his upper arm, who clearly couldn't care less about items like missing cutlery.

'That's not what I asked.'

'Are you from the police too?'

'No,' I said, but Hanna said, 'Yes, he is.' And to the waiter, who was at the most five or six years older than her, and whom she obviously liked, she added, 'He's a private detective – honest, he really is!' And she grinned as if that was a totally crazy notion.

'So you *are* from the police. They've been questioning us about that character upstairs all day already.' He also made no secret of the fact that he didn't like police officers.

I gave Hanna a look intended to tell her to keep her mouth shut. 'As she said: a private detective, not a policeman. And I don't know what character upstairs you mean. I'd simply like to know if you and the rest of the staff found there was a shashlik skewer missing at midday.'

'Why?'

'Because I found a skewer like that stuck in my car tyre just now, I have a racist neighbour who often plays tricks like that on me, and I found out by chance that he was eating here at midday. I don't want to see him in jail, I'd just finally like to pin something on him to get him to stop.'

'Racist neighbour?' repeated the waiter, looking at me more closely.

'He's Turkish,' explained Hanna, and I wondered if a daughter of my own would say that in just the same way.

The waiter said, in a distinctly more friendly voice, 'Okay, yes, there was a skewer missing at lunchtime, but I can't imagine it was your racist neighbour who nicked it.' He grinned a little uncertainly.

'Why not? Can you tell that just by looking at someone?'

'No, nonsense.' He hesitated. 'He was a nice guy, that's all. Left a good tip too – if he'd wanted to sabotage your tyre he wouldn't have nicked the cutlery to do it from the restaurant, I'm sure of that.'

'Can you describe him?'

The waiter looked at me for a moment. He doesn't like policemen, I remembered.

'Well, like I said, a nice guy. Age... sort of around fifty, I'm not so good at judging that kind of thing, comfortable clothes – like a professor or a nice teacher.'

'Are there any?' asked Hanna cheekily, and the waiter smiled at her. Then he went on, 'Anyway, man, we have so many customers in the middle of the day I can't notice everyone in detail, certainly not for a stupid fifty-cent skewer.'

'May I ask you something?' I took one of my business cards out of my jacket pocket. 'If you see him again, will you call me at this number?'

Taking my card, he glanced at it suspiciously. 'I thought this was about your neighbour? You can meet him any day, right? And like I said, the character I'm talking about wasn't the sort to stick skewers in car tyres.'

'You could be wrong. We've already agreed that you can't tell that kind of thing just by looking at people. Anyway, I'd like to confront my neighbour here in your café with the shashlik skewer that was sticking in my tyre. Of course he won't admit anything, but maybe it would give him a bit of a fright, and he'd leave me alone for a while.'

Then I put my hand in my jacket pocket again and paid for our thirteen-euro-eighty bill with a fifty-euro note. 'The change is for you so that you won't forget to call me.'

Surprised, he took the note and looked at my business card again. 'All this shit with your neighbour must really matter to you.'

'Any idea how much a new car tyre costs?'

He nodded. 'Okay, I'll call you. But like I said, I don't think…'

'Never mind that. Just call me if you see him.'

When we had risen from our table, Hanna said, 'Byeee' to him with a shamelessly long stare, and the jaw of the waiter roughly six years her senior dropped for a good moment. Shameless, but entirely innocent. I thought of Marieke and Valerie de Chavannes, and suddenly I understood why you would want to have a calculating old bastard killed if he exploited that mixture of shamelessness and innocence in your own daughter.

As we loaded my bike into the car boot, I said, 'Hey, suppose we ring your mama and ask if I can invite you to the cinema? There's a new Leo DiCaprio film.'

'Oh yes, I'd love that. My classes start late tomorrow morning.'

Chapter 8

Three days later Octavian called and told me that Abakay was denying everything. His friend Volker Rönnthaler had been visiting and he, Abakay, had left the apartment briefly to buy cigarettes. He returned to find Rönnthaler lying dead on the floor, and a man of Mediterranean appearance had attacked him without warning, kicked him and then tied him up and gagged him. He claimed to know nothing about the 'Autumn Flowers' file, saying someone must have planted it on him – someone who obviously wanted to destroy his life, probably the man who had attacked him and murdered his friend.

'Our computer expert can only prove that someone was interfering with the 'Autumn Flowers' file on the day of Rönnthaler's murder, and I assume that was you.'

'How about the list of girls' names that had the pseudonyms from 'Autumn Flowers' attached to it?'

'Also saved on the desktop by itself. Was never sent or received. It really does look like someone planted the file and the list on him.'

'And what about the girls themselves? Have you looked for them and found any of them?'

'Without surnames? Only one. I sent the photos to child

social services, and there was a reply about Lilly. Her father's under observation: he's a violent alcoholic, and Lilly has turned up at school with bruises a couple of times. The family lives in Praunheim. I've visited them. Lilly says she doesn't know Abakay, never set eyes on him. However, I'll go and see her again on her own. The old man was standing there the whole time, and the girl's obviously afraid of him. Anyway, not a situation in which a fourteen-year-old would admit to meeting older men.'

'In Praunheim. A Roma family, by any chance?'

'No idea. Why?'

'Just wondering. How about the heroin in the kitchen?'

'Also planted on him, Abakay says.'

'And who, in his opinion, is furious enough with him to stage such a show – murder, computer manipulation, drugs and the rest of it?'

'Hmm, well, he has two theories. For a start, he thinks his photos of the wretched state of things in Frankfurt will scare off potential investors in the city and thus infuriate the owners of buildings and land.'

'Come off it.'

'Yes, well. For instance, he published a series about the Gutleut district in the *Rundschau*, and in fact there really were some complaints to the editorial offices. You know the area well enough – run-down and close to the city centre, and building owners there have been waiting for years for the complications to be resolved and for a Starbucks or Häagen-Dazs or some such outfit to buy a place and set the ball rolling.'

'And kill someone on that account? Because of photos of beggars smoking. Have you recently taken to giving your suspects some grass to smoke while you interrogate them? What's the second theory?'

'That it's to do with his uncle.'

'The religious guy?'

87

'You know him?'

'I heard that he has an uncle who preaches in a mosque, that's all.'

'Hmm-hmm, Sheikh Hakim. Pretends to be crazy with talk of the holy war and so on, but as far as we know that's just for show and to take in idiots. Or maybe he does believe it, but he certainly believes in making money too. We suspect him of being big in the heroin trade, but we've never been able to prove anything. Abakay says he hasn't had anything to do with his uncle for a long time. But one of the phone calls he made from remand prison was to Sheikh Hakim's secretary.'

'What did he want the secretary to do?'

'Get him a lawyer.'

'And why would anyone kill Rönnthaler on account of Sheikh Hakim?'

'Abakay thinks it's a message: See what we could do to your nephew. This time we just killed the first guy we came across in his apartment and gave your nephew a good kicking in the balls, but next time... well, something along those lines. They couldn't get at Hakim himself. He always has bodyguards with him, his house is a fortress with garden walls two metres high, barred windows, CCTV cameras and God knows what else.'

'Where does he live?'

'In Praunheim.'

'Praunheim again. Maybe the sheikh is looking for little girls.'

'*One* little girl,' Octavian corrected me, 'and she lives at the other end of the district.'

'Great. And who, in Abakay's opinion, hates Hakim enough to kill someone who has nothing to do with any of it and beat up his nephew, just to get to him?'

'Abakay says some religious group, but if he knows anything at all about his uncle then he's really thinking that competitors in the drugs trade are behind it.'

'He doesn't think so, Octavian. I hope you realise, that's all nonsense. There was a fight between Rönnthaler and Abakay, Rönnthaler had the knife and Abakay had something thin and pointed that he used to kill him with. Your people just have to find that weapon. He probably threw it out of the window or into the stairwell just before I came into the apartment.'

'Hmm–hmm.'

'Meaning what?'

'We've searched every square centimetre of the apartment, the stairwell and the inner courtyard.' Octavian's tone was reserved. 'If there'd been a weapon anywhere there we'd have found it.'

'Maybe a dog snapped it up as a lolly. There was blood on it, after all.'

'Yes,' said Octavian. 'Or Abakay pushed it up his arse and that's why he's always shifting back and forth in his chair so cheerfully. Listen, Kemal, there are really only two possibilities. Either you're a suspect – and I can tell you that Abakay describes your outward appearance pretty well, and if we can find a clue to the identity of your client and establish a connection with her… I'm sure you'd never do a thing like that, but it's not out of the question that some colleague of mine might hit on the idea that you agreed to do some dirty work for the girl's parents.'

'What?'

'As you know, I have two daughters, aged twelve and fourteen. If I imagine anyone sending them out on the streets – I'd want to kill him myself. Maybe you came across Rönnthaler first, and then you felt a bit queasy because killing him had been too much for you, so you just beat up Abakay. As I said, I'm sure you'd never do a thing like that, but –'

He broke off. In my experience, 'I'm sure you'd never…' but meant 'I'm surely not sure that you'd never – and so I won't lift even a finger to help you.'

Interesting to learn within the space of a few days that no fewer than two people believed me capable of a contract killing.

'And the second possibility?'

'You'll be our witness. But first, I can't promise to keep your client out of it – if we find her she'll have a part to play in the trial, and to be honest with you I have some idea of her identity already. There were a photo and a business card among Abakay's papers: Valerie de Chavannes, Zeppelinallee – a big catch for someone like Abakay.'

'Never heard the name.'

'Well, that doesn't matter for now. Second, I have to warn you, if there's anything wrong with your story – for instance our doctor says that the cuts to Abakay's chest can hardly have been the result of a fight, and the knife wasn't lying in Rönnthaler's hand the right way for that – well, anyway, I hope that as an official witness you will give evidence that to some extent bears out the facts and the clues. In addition, and between you and me: if Sheikh Hakim has any kind of interest in his nephew, and in getting him out of jail before too long – I'm sure he knows people who can make life difficult for a main witness for the prosecution.'

An uncomfortable idea suddenly occurred to me. 'Listen, Octavian, you really don't want me as a witness, am I right?'

'I don't want a witness whose story is going to collapse in the course of the investigations or the trial. And then of course there's the fact' – he breathed in audibly – 'that people know we know each other, and that it will not do my career any good if an acquaintance of mine tries to lead the police astray.'

'But letting Abakay lead you astray is okay for your career?'

'Abakay is not an acquaintance of mine.'

'Well, Octavian, I'm sorry if it strikes you that I may have put you in an uncomfortable position, but…'

I was furious, and my sarcastic tone was childish. On the other hand, Octavian sounded very much as if Abakay had a chance of getting away with his version of events. Maybe I'd overdone my stage-setting in Abakay's apartment – too many inconsistencies, and in the end it would be my fault if they had to let Abakay go free. Whether he got two years or five years didn't matter so much to me, but I felt it would be scandalous for him to get off scot-free. So I said, without thinking any more of it, 'I'll volunteer to be a witness. And with the story you already know. That's what I saw. I'm not a doctor, how would I know whether Abakay's cuts came from a fight?'

'Abakay claims,' replied Octavian, 'that the man who attacked him also gave him those cuts.'

'I didn't attack him, I took him by surprise as he was bending over a man who had just been murdered, and then – doing the duty of any responsible citizen strong enough for it – I overpowered him and tied him up so that the police would have a chance of clearing up a crime. Because I thought that was what the police were for…'

'Okay, Kemal.'

'But if you'd rather believe Abakay! Why, for God's sake, would I cut his chest to pieces?'

'Well, for instance if you wanted it to look as if there's been a fight between Rönnthaler and Abakay.'

'For what reason?'

'I told you before: because you wanted to protect a suspect.'

'That's nonsense. When I entered the apartment Abakay already had his injuries, and all I did was tie him up and gag him.'

'And kick him brutally in the balls?'

'What else? Did I by any chance wreck his childhood too?'

'I'm only preparing you for what Abakay will accuse you of. So do I tell my colleagues that we have the man who handed Abakay over to us?'

'You have the witness, Octavian! You have the man who can prove that Abakay is a violent pimp who pumps underage girls full of heroin and sends them out on the streets.'

'Without giving the name of your client and her daughter?'

'At least I'll try to keep them both out of it as long as possible.'

'In case eventually that isn't possible, you should tell them about Sheikh Hakim. I know a great many people who prefer to save their own skin over the punishment of a criminal.'

'A good comment coming from a policeman.'

Octavian sighed. 'Oh, fuck you, Kemal. I'll be in touch.' And he ended the call.

I held the receiver for a while longer, and wondered if I had behaved particularly cleverly just now. In order to be able get myself out of this if the need arose, it was time to find Rönnthaler's murderer. So far I had no idea of his identity.

Then I searched the internet for Sheikh Hakim.

I found out nothing new. Crazy character, as Octavian had said. Although I found any degree of religious conviction crazy. Or as Slibulsky, who ran a chain of ice cream parlours and had recently shacked up with a woman twenty years younger than he was, and who was inspired equally by both Jesus and the Kabbala, put it, 'It's as if she goes into a shop made of thin air, orders seven scoops of vanilla ice cream, also consisting of thin air – seven because it's a lucky number – and smiles at the ice cream salesman who explains grimly that she'll get the scoops of ice cream later, when her pretty body has rotted in the ground. But the five euros she pays for the ice cream and the salesman's wallet into which they go are not just thin air.'

You couldn't tell from the internet sites whether Hakim was really as dangerous as Octavian had claimed. In photos the sheikh looked like an old man who bought his clothes in the secondhand shop on the ground floor of my office building, and spent a lot of time standing around in the street smoking with other old men. As far as I could tell from what I read, his views were nothing unusual for someone from his background. In an interview with the online newspaper *Euro Islam* he was asked all kinds of questions about everything under the sun, and he shared his thoughts on terrorism, suicide bombings, the Holy War, Islamism and so on with the usual, 'Terrible, but…' You had to look at the circumstances, said Sheikh Hakim, the historical background, the decades during which the West supported criminal despots, the sense of humiliation now turning into rage, particularly among the young, and of course Israel. In most studies of the Middle East, Israel was responsible for just about everything.

I had once suggested to Deborah, while we were watching a news item on the subject, that we could create our own Israel of sorts. We had quarrelled that afternoon. It began with the chaotic state of the apartment, or one of her girlfriends who got on my nerves, or Deborah's passion for work - even at the time I couldn't remember which - and ended as so often with 'antisocial Kayankaya' and 'ambitious Deborah who always has to show everyone what she can do' (i.e. that she had made it from Henningbostel and Mister Happy to the West End and Deborah's Natural Wine Bar, and would go much further yet). Anyway, I said, 'Now, if we had an Israel, when we felt a quarrel coming on we could always say: Hey, that damn Israel, that's why I never got around to tidying the place up. Or: It's only because of the bad influence of Israel that your friend Alexa is such a hysterical know-it-all. And even if we were simply tired, or the milk boiled over − it would be great to always have something to blame, and we'd see only each other's advantages and good points.'

Deborah looked at me as if I had something wrong with my upper storey.

'You might as well just say the Jews, only I suppose you don't dare.'

'I would dare, because it's a joke, darling. See what I mean? Not meant seriously. I was poking fun at the non-Jewish middle easterners. Only these days no one says it's the Jews' fault anymore. No anti-Semite in the world would say that now. He'd say: It's Israel's fault. So considering the technique of good jokes – if you believe, like me, that a joke is spicier the closer it comes to the truth – then in that case...'

'But I don't think that's at all funny.'

'Well, imagine we're watching news from the Middle East, and I said: Hey, how about we get ourselves a Jew, then we'll have someone to blame next time the milk boils over? You'd have thought that much less funny.'

'I don't think it's our day.'

Hmm, I thought, but if only we had an Israel...

'You know perfectly well that my granny...'

'Good heavens, what's she got to do with it?'

Deborah's granny – the real Deborah – had very probably been Jewish. Her grandfather had found her in 1945, starving, sick and ragged in the woods near Henningbostel, took her home with him, nursed her back to health and finally married her. She had never said anything about her origins or what had happened to her before 1945, but she had dropped a few hints, and there were certain questions that met with either an eloquent silence or a surprisingly harsh retort. When Deborah first told me about her granny ten years ago, I'd still been sceptical. What German girl, I thought, didn't have a Jewish granny these days? But then, in photographs of her, I saw a pale dark-haired beauty who wasn't typical of the North German countryside. It was from her that my Deborah had inherited her thick eyebrows, dark ringlets and full lips.

'Well, for me it does have something to do with it. I like jokes, but not on that subject, however funny they might be – and I said *might be*, get it? There's always something about them, you're supposed to think, Oh, how original, a forbidden subject but all the same, anyway. And they're not casual and effortless. And I think the more casual a joke, the funnier it is. For me, spiciness belongs in the soup. What's more – do I know how you really tick, deep down inside? Have we ever talked about that? You always say: Religion, no thanks – but I suppose your parents were Muslims, and you lived with your father until you were four, there must be some of that left...'

Oops! For a moment I must have looked taken aback. Having grown up in Frankfurt, never set foot in a mosque, never belonged to a union or a political party, never believed in anything but my own abilities, private detective, drinker, Mönchengladbach fan, and now, at the age of fifty-three, I hear the woman I've been having a relationship with for the last ten years come out with a remark like *I suppose your parents were Muslims*, all on account of my origins and a joke that she didn't understand.

My mother died in Turkey when I was born and my father took me with him to Germany, where he was run over by a post van four years later. I was put in a home, and two months later adopted by the Holzheims, a schoolmaster and a nursery school teacher. I have a few memories of my birth father. Mostly of the two of us sitting in a café, where he smoked and I drank apple juice. He treated me like an adult, not a small child. A lot of what he said I didn't understand, but I did realise that he respected me and wanted to be my best friend. Not my teacher. One thing he told me was: I can only teach you how to eat with a knife and fork, and you can teach me to know again whether the food really tastes good or just looks as if it does. That was the general gist of it anyway. My father spoke Turkish with me, a language that I soon forgot while living with the Holzheims. If my father had any religious feelings then they were about me. There were diary entries he had written that I later had translated, describing me as his 'great little miracle.' If Deborah was sensitive about

Jakob Arjouni

her granny, then I was at least as sensitive about my father. It got on my nerves that she classed him with the Muslims you saw on the TV news who hated all Jews.

'Well, now that you mention it... I've been thinking of asking if you can imagine wearing... well, not a veil all over your face, but up to your nose so that no man can see your wickedly tempting lips...'

And it might keep your mouth shut now and then.

Deborah looked at me, and then she suddenly said, in quite a friendly tone, 'Oh, come on, let's have a drink!' and went to the kitchen to get a bottle of wine. Alcohol standing in for the UN blue helmets. But after that we didn't quite trust ourselves to broach the subject again.

Sheikh Hakim's answer in his interview to the question of how, as an imam, he felt about alcohol and drugs was interesting: 'Well, that isn't really my field. But of course I know that all parts of the world have developed methods of relaxing after work at the end of the day. In South America they chew coca leaves, in Europe and my native land of Turkey they drink alcohol – but why are the means of relaxation used in other parts of the world criminalised here? First and foremost of course hashish, a relatively harmless herb. But smoking opium is a normal way to relax in many places. As a practising Muslim I do not drink alcohol or take any other drugs, but I am not blind. Alcoholism in Europe – just look at Russia – and the USA is an enormous problem. But have you ever heard of smoking hashish in the countries of North Africa or Asia leading to high mortality, a drop in the birth rate, and the devastation of large sections of the population? Do you know what I think? I think it's in the interests of the producers of alcohol not to allow any other legal alternative on the market, and as alcohol is mainly produced in the West one must, in my opinion, describe this state of affairs as extremely imperialistic.'

At least, it was interesting if Sheikh Hakim really was in the heroin trade. What a cheeky son of a bitch.

However, maybe Octavian and the police were wrong, and Hakim went to the expense of bodyguards and CCTV cameras just to impress his disciples. Anyway, the internet didn't seem to show that he was in any particular danger. On the contrary: Hakim appeared to be a rather conservative preacher, and not a genuinely deranged one. I could hardly imagine that he would protect a nephew gone bad who sent underage girls out on the streets. But then again: virgins, they had something with virgins, right? And unbelieving virgins - what about them? Could they be sent out on the streets maybe, as many of them as you liked? Maybe they even *ought* to be sent out on the streets? That was often the difficulty with religious people: ninety-nine per cent of the time religious people behaved relatively normally, but madness might lurk in the remaining one per cent. I don't mean like the pope, for instance, appearing in his pink paedo-slippers before the world, overpopulated as it is, to condemn condoms – the madness in that was out in the open. But take Hakim: decades of Western support for criminal despots, fair enough; feelings of humiliation now turning to rage, okay; legalise hashish, why not? But would he go so far as: maybe unbelieving virgins are the last scum of the earth for a righteous God!

I wondered how much of the news to pass on to Valerie de Chavannes. I had to warn her about Sheikh Hakim. And I had to warn her about the police. In both cases, moreover, I had to do so in my own interest. Unfortunately, Octavian was right: a mother who hires a private detective to free her daughter from the clutches of a dubious character, and then the dubious character accuses the private detective of first killing his friend who happened to be there and then beating him up – well, it didn't look good.

It's not out of the question that some colleague of mine might hit on the idea that you agreed to do some dirty work for the girl's parents.

And Valerie de Chavannes herself, three days earlier: *I'm wondering how far you would go...? For payment corresponding to the job, of course.*

I couldn't really count on her to maintain a persistent and convincing lie to the effect that she had never made the offer. Far from it. I was convinced that interrogation of any length by the police, or a nastier interrogation by Hakim's men, and she would throw them the morsel they wanted to get herself out of it as unscathed as possible. 'Okay, we did talk about it. Abakay... well, you know him. But of course I didn't mean it seriously. It was just a kind of fantasy, a game. But maybe Herr Kayankaya... I hardly know him, but he was very committed, and I think he also liked me a lot...'

Yes, I could probably count more on something of that nature.

So I had to convince Valerie de Chavannes to deny any connection whatsoever with me to whoever might ask, and do it without frightening her. I didn't want her turning in panic to the police. And I wanted to leave her believing that the evidence against Abakay was still rock-solid. No excitement, everything was going just fine, Kayankaya held the reins firmly in hand.

I tapped Valerie de Chavannes's number into my phone. As it rang, I caught myself thinking of her slender feet in those silver sandals.

'De Chavannes.'

'Hello, Kayankaya here. Everything okay with you?'

'I wouldn't put it quite like that, but nothing has happened, if that's what you mean.'

Her tone was cool – as cool as a tone could be without sounding openly hostile. Did she bear me a grudge for giving her the brush-off when she wanted to hire me to commit murder? Or was it simply the usual de Chavannes tone? I remembered that she'd sounded like that at the start, when we first met.

'Yes, that's what I meant. How is Marieke?'

'I don't know. She seems really upset, as if she were in shock. She won't talk to me. Sits in her room all day listening to Jack Johnson.'

'Well, that would upset me as well.'

When Hanna did odd jobs for Deborah in the wine bar she always brought Jack Johnson music with her. She thought it was the sort of music that was also bound to appeal to adults who drink red wine.

'Very funny.'

'I'm trying. I had the feeling that Marieke is a strong character, the sort who doesn't go under so easily.'

'And she doesn't. But if she does then she *really* goes under.'

'I'm sorry.'

'But that's not why you called.'

'No. I wanted to tell you that the police – that is, well, the officer responsible for the Abakay case – has named me as a witness in his records, although I got him to promise to keep my name out of it. Well, he knows me and he doesn't particularly like me, so he took his opportunity to do me a bad turn.'

'Why would he do you a bad turn that way?'

'Because, of course, sooner or later the question of who I was working for will come up. The court will want to know what I was doing in Abakay's apartment, and Abakay's lawyers will do their best to make me look like an unreliable witness – they'll say my client paid me to smear Abakay's reputation, and so I thought something up. Well, not many clients want to be named in a criminal case – I assume you're not among the few exceptions – and no private detective likes it to be known that he can't protect his clients' names. So I'd like to ask you, if anyone comes to see you in connection with

Abakay, to deny having any contact with me. If you've made a note of my name anywhere, or my business card is lying about the house, get rid of it.'

'You mean someone might break into our house?' Her tone was still cool. Maybe too cool. As if, after all that had happened, a mere burglary held no terrors for her. Perhaps it really didn't. All the better.

'No, but a halfway tricky private detective who knows his business could pretend to be someone from the municipality and sniff about your house, or he could invite your housekeeper for a coffee and get her to tell him everything about recent visitors. So it would be a good thing if your housekeeper doesn't come upon my name when she was clearing your wastepaper baskets.'

'I see... okay.'

She paused, and suddenly it seemed to me as if I were on a different line. I heard her breathing: a heavy, hasty, slightly tremulous struggle for breath. I had never heard anything like it except in people suffering a panic attack or before a very unpleasant and very important encounter. Like de Chavannes always sounded...

'Ought I to worry about Marieke?'

'No more than I suppose you're worrying anyway, after what happened. Abakay's lawyers will try to find witnesses to let him off the hook, and if all Marieke and Abakay really talked about was photography and social injustice, then of course she'd be perfect.'

'If,' repeated Valerie de Chavannes, pausing again. And once again I heard her breathing. But I didn't think she was breathing so heavily because of our phone call. I had thought, once before, that underneath the various masks worn by Valerie de Chavannes there was nothing but a constant state of fear. The arrogant upper-class cow, angry and scornful, the little woman in need of help, the yearning, melting tattooed minx de Chavannes, and now the Agent 007 Mama

100

preserving a cool head in difficult times and keeping the show on the road – all of them camouflage and attempts to stay largely unscathed. And that had nothing to do with Abakay; it had always been like that, I thought – or, anyway, for a long time.

'You still haven't told me what exactly the crime was that Abakay committed. Did you mean it about murder, or was that just to scare me?'

'Both. Whether he committed the murder himself isn't certain, but he's certainly involved in it. However, that's nothing to do with Marieke. Abakay is a little street mongrel who will try to pick up a few euros where and when he can. Of course drugs play a part, and probably stolen cars, weapons, forged papers, God knows what. And here we come very close to a capital crime. All the same, he did take those photos on the side, and that's what linked him to Marieke.'

'Of course you know that I'd love to believe you.'

'Of course I do. But tell me a reason I'd lie to you.'

She hesitated. 'Because you don't want to hurt me.' She was trying to keep the cool tone of voice going, but it didn't entirely work. Or she acted as if she were trying to keep the cool tone of voice going, and let it slip into emotion on purpose.

'I really would be very reluctant to hurt you, but I wouldn't tell you fairy tales on that account.'

'How do you explain Marieke's behaviour over the last few days?'

'Well, my bet would be she feels crossed in love. I didn't say the photos were all of it. And Abakay certainly knows how to impress a sixteen-year-old. Anyway, if I were you I'd make sure Marieke doesn't go prison visiting in the immediate future.'

'For God's sake!'

'You should be glad she's spending all day in her room. Maybe you should buy her a different CD.'

For a moment there was silence on the line. Obviously her breathing had calmed down, or she was holding the receiver to one side. Then she sighed, sounding surprisingly amused, and asked, 'How old are you?'

'Fifty-three. Why?'

'Because no one buys CDs these days. They download music to their MP3 players.'

'I even still have some cassettes.'

'Simply Red or something like that, I expect.'

'No, Whitney Houston. But I can't listen to the cassettes anymore, my recorder's broken.'

'Whitney Houston,' she repeated, and was about to say something making fun of me – it wasn't difficult to make fun of people who still listened to Whitney Houston – but then something seemed to occur to her and she suddenly fell silent.

So did I. Probably we had both carried on like that because we were glad to get away from the subject of Abakay for a moment. But in no time at all we had landed in front of an open door. For instance, she went on: Whitney Houston – right, now I do believe you're fifty-three. What else do you like? Foreigner? Münchner Freiheit? And I: You've never listened to Whitney Houston properly. At three in the morning, with a few beers or something else inside you, windows of the bar open, mild air, and then 'The Greatest Love of All' on the jukebox – you could fall on your knees with happiness. And she again: Well, okay. I have a recorder that still works... Or something like that. Anyway, we both knew that from here to a Whitney Houston evening together with wine and candlelight it was three more sentences at the most.

Finally I said, 'Apart from which my Whitney Houston days are over.'

She cleared her throat, and her tone became friendly but objective. 'Well, I hope so, at the age of fifty-three.'

'You mean fifty-three is too old for Whitney Houston?'

'Too old for Whitney Houston period, I'd say. A song now and then, why not?'

I noticed that I was baring my teeth. 'I bet you've listened to a Whitney Houston song now and then on your MP3 player.'

She hesitated. 'Could be. I don't know. It's a long time since I listened to any music at all.'

It was on the tip of my tongue to say: Surely a ballad or so with Abakay now and then?

Instead, I said, 'It'll come back. These are just phases.' And then, more briskly, 'Did you get my bill?'

'Yes.' A short pause, then back to the cool tone. 'Do I destroy that as well?'

'Don't transfer the money direct to me anyway. I'll collect it in cash sometime.'

She didn't reply.

'Or maybe I'll send a friend to collect it.'

'Yes, let's do it that way,' she said.

It annoyed me. I didn't want her letting me go so quickly. And it annoyed me that it annoyed me.

'Okay, we'll do it that way. And please let me know at once if anyone asks you about me.'

'Can't I tell your friend? Wouldn't that be simpler?'

I looked at my big station clock, behind which my pistols, handcuffs, knock-out drops and pepper spray were hidden. 'No, it wouldn't be simpler, because my friend has no idea what this is about.'

'Fine, then, I'll call you. Anything else we ought to discuss?'

I said no, we said goodbye and hung up. I was furious. With her, with myself. And briefly I wondered how, after Whitney Houston, I had gotten to Foreigner and Münchner Freiheit. Brothel music, all of it.

I was still sitting thoughtfully at my desk when Katja

Lipschitz called ten minutes later.

'Hello, Herr Kayankaya.'

'Hello, Frau Lipschitz.'

'I've spoken to our publisher. If you're still prepared to do the job I'd like to hire you as bodyguard for Malik Rashid for three days at the Book Fair.'

'Yes, I'm ready to do it. Did you tell your publisher my fee? We don't want problems about it later.'

I didn't know why, probably it was just a cliché picked up from cheap TV films. But I thought there could be some difficulty in meeting financial obligations in the book trade.

'It's all decided. Send me your contract by email.'

'I'll do that at once. The advance is a minimum daily fee, a thousand euros plus taxes. As soon as that's in my account I'll take a look at Rashid's hotel. What was its name again?'

'The Harmonia in Niederrad.'

'When does Rashid arrive?'

'At noon on Friday, is that all right for you? Midday Friday until midday on Monday, three days?'

'That's okay. Shall I fetch him from the airport or the railway station?'

'No, my assistant will do that. Rashid, you and I will meet at twelve at the hotel to discuss everything. From then on he'll be in your care.'

'Fine. See you at twelve on Friday, then.'

'I have one request, Herr Kayankaya. It's possible that journalists will approach you during the Fair. Rashid and his novel will be much discussed, so his bodyguard could be a subject of interest as well. Have you read his book, what you think of it as a Muslim, and so on...'

'And you'd like me to keep my mouth shut.'

'Well, what you told me about your attitude towards religion, and your manner in general... don't misunderstand me, I thought it was very... interesting to talk to you, but... you see, journalists don't like anything complicated. And a

Turkish bodyguard who compares God to hot stones and possibly doesn't take the man he's guarding, an internationally famous author who is generally considered to have written a very important and sensational book, well, possibly doesn't take him entirely seriously – anyway, it wouldn't be simple to get that across. And then the papers might say: best-selling author mocked by own bodyguard, or something like that.'

'Don't worry. I'm not at all interested in getting into the papers.'

'That's what I thought. I just wanted to warn you – some journalists can be very pushy.'

'Thanks.'

'And something else...'

'Yes?'

'In Rashid's daily schedule you'll see what events he's taking part in. One of them is a panel discussion at the House of Literature with Dr Breitel...'

She paused, giving me time to react, and when I said nothing she went on to explain, 'One of the editors of the *Berliner Nachrichten.* The title is "The Ten Plagues..."' Another pause for my reaction. 'It's out of the Bible, when God sent plagues of heat, locusts, hail and so on into the country... Oh, I don't remember all of it. Anyway, the discussion will turn on the various threats to Western society: falling birth rates, families breaking up, isolation, excessive technology, the internet, a few more things, and finally – with Malik Rashid as the guest, of course the real subject behind all this is whether there isn't an increasingly well-organised Islam behind it all, preparing the threats, that's to say the plagues, more or less intentionally. For instance, there'll be the consequences of the falling birth rate among, er...'

'Us,' I said, helping her out.

'Yes, us, and the rising birth rate among...'

'Immigrant families.'

'Thanks, it'll go something like that. Sorry, not a subject I know very well, and I can't find my notes about it at the moment.'

'Do you remember what it said about Islam overwhelming us with excessive technology?'

'Well, it was to do with the internet. I think Dr Breitel is going to say that the internet is the real engine of destruction in our society because – oh, look, here are my notes and they say "it creates lonely, frustrated, dehumanised creatures who can no longer function in a society unable to defend itself." And lower down: "Do we know how much Arab and Iranian oil money has gone into the World Wide Web? From a region where the majority of the population doesn't own computers? Is the internet a drug with which the rulers and religious leaders of the East are swamping the Western world to make us a crowd of couch potatoes stuffed with useless knowledge and satiated with pornography? Is the internet perhaps nothing but an intelligent means of warfare? Just as the British weakened China in the nineteenth century from within with opium, then overthrew it by military means?" And so on… We're looking forward to a controversial evening. Questions from the audience will be allowed at the end; we're asking for them to be sent to our home page for security reasons. Driss Mararoufi, head chef at the Tunisian Medina restaurant in Sachsenhausen, will provide refreshments.' Katja Lipschitz paused for a moment and then proclaimed, in rather too loud a voice, as if to drown out any possible doubts: 'It will certainly be a very interesting evening.'

'It certainly will. But what did you really want to tell me?'

'Oh… yes. Well, as I said, we're asking for questions in advance for security reasons. In fact, it's not open to the general public, but we didn't want to make that obvious. People are more likely to buy books at occasions where they couldn't get tickets than at those they weren't expected to attend. The risk of letting in all and sundry was just too great. The mayor of Frankfurt is coming, maybe even the Hessian minister of the interior... well, anyway, in that connection I wanted to ask you to wear... well, suitable clothing.'

'How do you mean? A turban?'

'No, of course not.' She gave a brief, nervous laugh. 'If you have a suit, or at least a smart jacket... it will be a very exclusive evening, and in your own interest... I assume you wouldn't like to be the only one in jeans and a corduroy jacket.'

'Thanks for the helpful hint. Is a blue pin-striped suit okay?' I thought of Slibulsky, who had once called blue pin-striped suits the monastic garb of all disreputable folk such as Turks. But obviously Katja Lipschitz wasn't familiar with this association.

'Wonderful,' she said, pleased. Then her tone of voice suddenly became slightly troubled. 'And I'd like to point out one more thing that can – well, can be surprising for people who don't know him or the book trade. Er... Dr Breitel likes to wear short trousers, even in the evening and anywhere, I mean...'

'He does? Even in winter?'

'With knee-high socks.'

'Well, what a good thing you persuaded me not to wear my cord jacket. That would have been a real faux pas!'

'Er, yes...'

'Would you like me to wear short trousers as well?'

'For heaven's sake, no – that's Dr Breitel's privilege, so to speak. His own signature style, if you see what I mean.'

'I do. May one pay him compliments? On the fabric, the cut of the trousers, maybe on his legs?'

'No, no, please don't. Just try not to notice.'

'Okay.'

'Dr Breitel is...' I liked the way she obviously had to overcome her embarrassment '...very important. If you want to sell books, I mean.'

'I do indeed see what you mean, Frau Lipschitz. Don't worry, I won't do anything to attract attention.'

'Thank you very much, Herr Kayankaya. Sometimes it isn't entirely easy...' She was searching for words.

'Exactly,' I said.

'Yes. Well, yes. Anyway, I'll send you the schedule for those three days with the signed contract, and a pass to the Book Fair.'

'And the threatening letters.'

'Oh, yes, the threatening letters. Of course.'

'I'll see you on Friday next week, then.'

'Friday next week, Herr Kayankaya, thanks.'

Chapter 9

The advance payment came into my account at the end of the week, and by post I received the signed contract, Rashid's schedule for his visit to Frankfurt, and a pass to the Book Fair. No threatening letters. Those were either a pure invention or a ridiculous insult, but in any case nothing that Katja Lipschitz could show me or wanted to show me. And fundamentally it made no difference. Rashid was getting a bodyguard for promotional purposes. A Gregory job. As long as Maier Verlag was paying.

On the Monday I visited the Harmonia Hotel. A typical middle-class dump with worn fitted carpets; cheap and brightly coloured sofas; little halogen lamps; a bar with beer, spirits and cheese crackers; and a collection of signed postcards on the wall from B-list celebrities who had once stayed at the Harmonia. I bought a bad espresso and got the waiter to show me the back door and the emergency exits. 'Because of my father. He might be staying a couple of days here next month, and he's terrified of fire.'

On Tuesday I made my official statement on the Abakay case to the police.

On Wednesday I had a call at the office from a man called

Methat who said he was Sheikh Hakim's secretary. He began
by speaking Turkish, until he gave me a moment to explain
that I'd never learnt the language. After an incredulous pause,
a Turkish curse – at least, it sounded Turkish – and a few
contemptuous lip-smacking sounds, he finally went on in
German with a strong Hessian accent, and I had to ask three
times before I got his drift, which was that His Magnificence
wanted to see me.

'Who wants to see me?'

'Is Nificence.'

'Munificence?'

'No, no! Nificence!

'Sorry, try again.'

'Is Nificence! Like nificent view!'

'Ah, I get it. His Magnificence.'

'Don't pretend you…!'

'Er… who is His Magnificence?'

'I ave said I am secretary of Sheisch Hakim!'

'Okay. Then please tell Sheisch Hakim that if he wants to
see me he'd better make an appointment by phone or email.
He'll find my address in the Yellow Pages. I'm travelling a lot
just now and I'm only occasionally in my office.'

'You must be crazshy!'

He was getting on my nerves. 'I assure you I'm not,' I said,
in as heavy a Hessian dialect as I could manage. 'But I'm
bizshy! So tell him to make an appointment, saying what it's
about. As I said, I'm busy at the moment and I have to hang
up.'

I cut the connection before he could call me any more
names.

So it was only one day before Sheikh Hakim heard of my
statement to the police. I decided that when I got the chance
I would tell Octavian that not only did he 'know a great
many people who prefer to save their own skin over the
punishment of a criminal', he also had at least one officer at

police HQ who preferred a small fortune in cash, a bag of heroin, a free visit to a brothel or some other inducement within Hakim's or Abakay's reach to the punishment of the said criminals. I firmly believed that Octavian did not know who it was, or who they were, but someone was keeping Sheikh Hakim up to date. I didn't believe quite so firmly that he would do anything to unmask the person or persons concerned. It probably depended on what height he or they had reached in the pyramid of police power. When Octavian took me to the door after I'd made my statement the day before, his quiet words of farewell had been, 'You're doing this at your own risk, I hope you realise that. When all this is over, we can see each other again, but until then I guess we'd better not. My promotion will be decided in the next few weeks.'

'I tell you what, Octavian, maybe we'd better not see each other again, full stop.'

'Oh, don't come over like that! I'd get another thousand a month, and I have family to support in Romania.'

'Don't we all?' I said.

'You don't,' he said coolly.

'I've seen the girls in Abakay's catalogue. They're my Romanian family.'

'Don't turn sentimental.'

'Is it sentimental to feel ill when I think of thirteen-year-olds on sale for fucking? Is it sentimental to want to nail the man who's offering them? You've been in the Vice Squad too long, Octavian, it's bad for your morals.' And with that we left each other without further goodbyes and went our separate ways.

On Thursday Valerie de Chavannes tried to reach me on my mobile. I was sitting in the wine bar with Deborah, eating tripe sausage, drinking red wine and reading the sports pages, and the first time the phone rang I ignored the call, the second time too. Then she sent a text message: *Please call back as soon as you can! Urgent! Danger!* I finished my sausage, emptied my glass, went into the little courtyard behind the wine bar and called back.

Valerie de Chavannes answered at once.

'Herr Kayankaya! At last!' Her voice was shaking, and sounded nasal, as if she'd been shedding tears. Now and then I heard her breathing heavily again as she struggled for air.

'What's the matter, Frau de Chavannes?'

'A man called Methat rang just now! Had I set a private detective on Abakay?'

'And what did you say?'

'What you told me to say – I said I didn't know what he was talking about.'

'Did he believe you?'

'No idea. He threatened me!' She struggled for air. 'He said if I'd hired you then I must get you to withdraw your evidence against Abakay as quickly as possible or my daughter's life would be in danger!'

Maybe it was because I imagined that sentence coming from Methat in his heavy Hessian dialect – life in danscher - but anyway, I didn't take the threat as seriously as I probably should have done when talking to Valerie de Chavannes. I said, 'Oh yes?'

'What do you mean, oh yes? I told you Abakay would still be dangerous even in prison!'

'Well, then you must decide: either you want him in prison or you don't.'

'You know exactly where I want him!'

She spoke from the heart, furious, resentful, implying: I told you that you ought to kill him!

'Take it slowly. We're talking on the phone, there could be someone listening in. And after all, I'm a witness in a murder case – so don't say anything that might be misunderstood. Of course *I* know that you want to see him *in prison…*'

A pause, more heavy breathing.

I didn't really think that the police were listening in on me

or Valerie de Chavannes, but the thought of a bugged phone
– *you know exactly where I want him!* – made me feel queasy for
a moment.

After a while, regaining some measure of control over
herself, she said, 'And now what? What do we do?'

'Well, Frau de Chavannes, *we* don't do anything.
Remember? You hired me to bring your daughter home.'

'Oh, and now you're wriggling out of it like a coward!'

'You're welcome to ask me to take on another job for you
– protecting your daughter, or you, or both of you. But I'm
convinced that the best and also the cheapest thing I can do
for you at the moment is not to show myself near you.'

'That's what you said last time!'

'Because it was true last time. I suggest the following. You
tell Marieke's school that she'll be absent, sick, for another
week, and you stay at home with her. If Methat rings again,
or the police, or anyone else, don't let them persuade you to
do anything. No one but you and I know about our
connection. Even Marieke knows only a police officer called
Magelli. If someone rings the doorbell, don't open the door,
and if that someone doesn't go away, then call me. If you're
still being pestered in a week's time, I'll deal with it.'

Once again she drew a huge breath, as if a sack of plaster
lay on her chest, before she cautiously asked, 'Is that a
promise?'

'It is.'

'Please, Herr Kayankaya… I really am so frightened, and
I'm all on my own…'

'I said I'll deal with it. But you have to hold out for that
week. I'm sure that at the moment Abakay's people are just
poking about at random. Presumably Abakay has drawn up a
list of people to whom he's done wrong in some way or
another, and who he correctly assumes could have hired a
private detective to kick his legs from under him. You were
probably just one name among many. So again: deny ever

having heard of me and I bet that in a couple of days' time they'll leave you alone.'

She sighed. 'My God, Herr Kayankaya, what a mess I've got myself into.' And after a pause, 'I'm sorry, I'm being a nuisance to you, aren't I?'

'Oh, never mind that.'

She stopped for a moment and then laughed quietly, in a familiar way, as if we were friends of many years' standing and she was glad that I was still the same old roughneck I used to be.

'May I ask you something?'

'Of course.'

'Do you think…' She hesitated. Or she pretended to be hesitating. Or both. Probably Valerie de Chavannes herself no longer knew what she did unintentionally and what was calculation or a trick. Anyway, her hesitation gave the question the clarity of which she then tried to deprive it – or made out she was trying to deprive it – by adopting a tone as objective as possible and slightly pert, adding a barely perceptible pinch of girlish flirtatiousness. 'Do you think we'd ever have met without all this?'

This time I was the one to hesitate.

'Before I answer that question, may I just tell you the name of the friend who will collect my fee from you in the next few days? He's Ernst Slibulsky. You can open the door to him, please.'

'Ernst Slibulsky, okay.'

'Maybe we have in fact met before,' I went on, pausing again and thinking that I sensed her holding her breath at the other end of the line. It was a shot in the dark, but since our first meeting I couldn't shake off that thought. Not that I thought we had really got to know each other, but maybe we had been around in the same place at the same time.

'You left home when you were sixteen, and there aren't many places in Frankfurt where a young girl who's run away like that can get by somehow or other. How old are you now?'

She didn't reply. But probably not because she wanted to conceal her age from me, more likely because she scented danger.

'Come on – you look as if you are in your mid-thirties, but you're not. Mid-forties?'

For a moment I thought she'd put down the receiver, but then I heard her breathing.

'Let's say around forty. Marieke is sixteen, and you weren't silly enough to get pregnant too young. In your late twenties, I'd assume, when your wild days were gradually coming to an end. Work it out like that, and about twenty-five years ago you were standing with a travelling bag or a rucksack at the end of Zeppelinallee on the Bockenheimer Warte. Maybe you then spent a few weeks with friends, or on holiday in the south of France or somewhere like that, but in the course of time your friends went back to school and you'd come to the end of your money. Of course you'd sooner have cut off an arm than ask your parents for financial support, or even go back home. Well, at the time I was out and about in the railway station district on both professional and private business...'

She cut the connection. Maybe she thought my assumptions were simply insulting; or alternatively I'd hit the bull's-eye. You had to have – like Deborah did - a certain kind of North German composure and toughness that comes of living in that bleak, flat countryside to be proud of having survived the sex clubs and striptease bars of the station area. For a banker's daughter and wife of an artist, a part of her life spent in the best known and (at that time) the deepest gutter in Frankfurt was probably not a subject on which she wanted to dwell.

And suddenly an uncomfortable thought came to me. How old, in fact, was Abakay? Mid-thirties, I assumed, but then it didn't compute. But at least symbolically he could have conjured up ghosts of Valerie de Chavannes's past in the station area, if there had been any. And perhaps she hadn't minded that at first. Now over forty, married with a child, living in a villa, weekends spent at health spas, sushi suppers, Woody Allen films – you liked remembering your own youth, however bizarre it was. But then suppose memory became the present, the pimp comes into your own house, gets to know your sixteen-year-old daughter...

I wanted to get back, quickly, to the wine bar and my unsentimental Jewish Frisian girlfriend. Deborah took life as a learning curve, or rather a learning staircase. Once she was up one step she climbed the next, and she never went back. Why learn something twice? She would have spotted a pimp at first sight, never mind his disguise as a photographer and a man out to improve the world, and would have chased him off with her broom. Valerie de Chavannes's neediness made me nervous.

'Oh, there you are. Could you please bring a couple of cartons up from the cellar, twelve bottles of Foulards Rouges in each?'

Deborah was kneeling behind the bar in her short blue denim skirt, checking on the provisions in the fridge. It was just before five, and the wine bar would soon be filling up.

I inspected her bare legs. 'Are we going to empty one of those bottles ourselves?'

She looked up, shot me a quick glance to see if I was drunk, then smiled her clever, mischievous smile, which said clearly: Listen, you, I'm at work! And she added, for fun, 'Your place or mine?'

'Yours, dear heart. You know what my wife is like...'

'Sure, she'd get on anyone's nerves. Coming home in the middle of the night, wanting to tell you what her day in the bar was like, dropping off to sleep at once on the sofa or in an armchair, and then she has to be undressed and put to bed.

I can tell you, my old man is quite a handful too. He's been going to bed earlier and earlier since he stopped smoking. And when we want to cuddle or at least see the nightly news on TV, he's snoring fit to burst our eardrums.'

I shook my head. 'What rotten luck. Well, nothing to be done about it. All the same,' I added, jerking my chin at her legs, 'nice skirt.'

'Thanks. Will you pick me up later?'

'I'll set the alarm.'

'And I'll have a double espresso last thing.'

She winked at me and turned back to the fridge. On my way through the backyard and down a damp flight of brick steps to the cellar, I thought about those ghosts of the past conjured up for me by Valerie de Chavannes. And how seductive such ghosts could be. I wasn't Deborah, I knew I could go down those steps again at any time, all the way to the very bottom, and then, at the age of fifty-three, start all over again: spirits, cigarettes, sleepless nights, anger, the light on the horizon.

I decided not to keep my promise. I wasn't going to deal with anything or anyone for Valerie de Chavannes next week, not even if Sheikh Hakim's entire congregation were to come up Zeppelinallee on their knees. And the danger of being suspected of a contract killing in the true sense of the term? Well, I thought I now knew who had killed Rönnthaler. I didn't have the evidence yet, but I'd soon find it. And then Valerie de Chavannes could tell the police anything she liked.

I wanted to think not about her but about Deborah and our Christmas holidays. Over Christmas the wine bar would be closed for a full week, and Slibulsky had told me about a good spa hotel in Alsace.

Here we go, I thought, picking up the two cases. Twenty-four bottles of Foulards Rouges, Frida – my favourite wine, and not just mine; it was excellent. I had learnt a lot from

Deborah about wine, and other things too. But I also still knew: beer with a chaser of spirits and Whitney Houston on the jukebox could be a lot of fun.

Chapter 10

On Friday I met Malik Rashid and Katja Lipschitz in the midst of a dreary dance of colour. The lounge of the Harmonia Hotel had yellow and pink chessboard pattern carpeting, Rashid was sitting on a lime-green sofa, and Katja Lipschitz in a faded blue wing chair. In front of them stood a table with a black top and a metal frame, and on it were orange half-litre mugs with milky white foam rising from them.

Katja Lipschitz, legs crossed and arms folded, sat leaning back, with her head almost horizontally to one side, as if to disguise the difference in size between herself and Rashid like that. Or maybe she was just dozing off.

Rashid, upright, legs apart, was talking to her and gesticulating wildly. He was wearing bright white trainers, jeans and a beige T-shirt bearing the legend *The old words are the best, and short words are the best of all*. He had a thin face with fine features, lively eyes always moving around and an amused expression, as if to say: Yes, my dear, what a crazy, confused world, what luck there are fellows like me around to keep on top of it.

Rashid didn't look up until I stopped a couple of metres in front of him, and his expression of amusement instantly turned to a certain reluctance. Perhaps he thought I was a member of the hotel staff.

'Yes?'

'Hello, my name is Kayankaya.'

'Oh,' said Katja Lipschitz, raising her head. Now she clearly towered above Rashid. 'I didn't see you coming.'

And Rashid cried, 'Aha!' and switched instantly to an expression of radiance. He rose from the sofa, spreading his arms wide in a theatrical manner. 'My protector! Greetings!'

Katja Lipschitz didn't seem to know whether to stand up too. On the one hand there was civility to me, on the other she was probably thinking of Rashid's feelings. I noticed at once that she was wearing flat-heeled shoes, but if she stood right beside him Rashid was still going to look like a gnome. Or she was going to look like a giant – perhaps it was that more than anything that she wanted to avoid.

'Don't get up,' I said to Katja Lipschitz, offering Rashid my hand. 'Pleased to meet you, Herr Rashid.'

'Oh!' He lowered his arms and ironically mimed disappointment. 'So formal, my friend! How are we to spend three days cheek by jowl like that?'

I glanced at Katja Lipschitz, who was smiling as if her boss had just put a farting cushion on her chair.

I left my hand in midair. 'Cheek by jowl.'

'Or bristle by bristle.' He grinned, glad of his little coup. 'Because, aren't we all little pigs somewhere deep down inside? Or sometimes big pigs. Maybe that's why we don't eat them, it would be a kind of cannibalism.' He grinned a little more cheerfully, before turning apologetically to Katja Lipschitz. 'Excuse me, Katja, by *we* I meant us Orientals. I've no objection to eating pork, but *I* don't eat it. And that's nothing to do with religion. The Jews – and Jews are Orientals too, right? A fraternal people. And what are the bloodiest wars?' He pointed his index finger questioningly at me. I withdrew my proffered hand and put it in my trouser pocket.

'Wars between brothers! Anyway – the Jews don't eat pork either. Nor do Christians in the Orient – and many of my best friends are Christians,' he added, laughing. 'At least, they've never served me ham hock!'

Katja Lipschitz joined in his laughter, whether out of professionalism or because she really thought it funny I couldn't tell.

I said, 'Herr Rashid, I am to be your bodyguard for three days. We shall probably be sitting in the same restaurant several times, maybe at the same table. Please let me know whether it will bother you if I order sausage.'

For a moment his eyes rested on me as if he were wondering whether it had really been a good idea to pick me as his bodyguard.

Then he shook himself, his mouth stretched in a smile, and all at once he was my new best friend again, beaming radiantly. 'I've already heard that you have your own opinions and' – he nodded approvingly – 'defend them in your own original way.'

Once again I glanced at Katja Lipschitz. This time she was smiling as if her boss had put a board studded with nails on her chair.

'Well, Herr Rashid, if eating sausage is an opinion – yes, I have opinions. Shall we discuss the rest of your day? I assume you'll have to turn up at the Fair to meet your fans and carry out your engagements.'

He laughed ironically, clearing his throat. 'Ah, my fans! I'm only a little scribbler. Now Hans Peter Stullberg has fans – so does Mercedes García…' And in a tone of casual interest, glancing at Katja Lipschitz across the multicoloured seating and the chessboard pattern of the carpet, 'I wonder, what hotel are they staying in?'

For a moment Katja Lipschitz seemed to be in danger of

blushing. She caught herself just in time, assumed a kindly smile and explained, 'Her Spanish publisher is looking after Mercedes García. I believe she's staying in a guestroom at the Instituto Cervantes. And luckily we were able to get a room at the Frankfurter Hof at the last moment for Hans Peter Stullberg. Rohlauf Verlag kindly let us have one of their quota. On account of his age and his back trouble, Hans Peter Stullberg can't walk long distances these days.'

'Oh, the poor man.' Rashid twisted his face into an expression of sympathy.

'Yes, he really doesn't have an easy time. In addition,' Katja went on, with what I thought was a tiny, cunning flash in her eyes, 'the Frankfurter Hof would have been out of the question for you, for reasons of security. Thousands of people are going in and out of the hotel every evening and every night during the Book Fair.' And she explained, for my benefit, 'The bar of the Frankfurter Hof could be described as the unofficial centre of the air after ten in the evening. Everyone meets there: authors, publishers, journalists, agents, editors.'

'Apart from which,' said Rashid, also turning to me, 'the Frankfurter Hof is, of course, greatly overestimated as a hotel. Last time I stayed there during the Book Fair –' He suddenly stopped. Perhaps he sensed Katja Lipschitz suddenly looking at the floor, rather exhausted. 'Well, never mind. Average food, unfriendly service – that's what you usually get at the so-called best hotels in the city. They don't need to go to any trouble. Why don't we sit down, my friend?'

'Let's do that,' I agreed.

'Would you like something to drink?' asked Katja Lipschitz.

'Mineral water, please.'

As she signalled to the barman, Rashid returned to his subject. 'Of course there are exceptions. At the Literature Festival in New York last year –'

'Herr Rashid,' I interrupted him, 'it's twelve thirty, and at one thirty, according to your schedule, you have your first engagement at the Fair. I'd like to discuss a couple of details with you first.'

'I understand.' He laughed. 'My good German Kemal – work is work, and schnapps is schnapps!' He laughed again. In fact, he seemed glad that I'd stopped him talking about hotels.

I said, 'First and foremost it's about the technicalities when we're together. For instance, when we're moving through the halls of the Fair, I'd like to decide, depending on the situation and the number of people present, whether I go behind you or ahead of you. If there are cameras turned on you, of course I'll keep in the background.'

Perhaps it was the idea of clicking cameras, perhaps the memory that I had not been hired by the publishing house for my social skills but to protect him from any deranged fanatics – anyway, his facial expression suddenly turned positively solicitous. He nodded, and said, 'Of course, you must do everything that you think right.'

Katja Lipschitz backed this up. 'Herr Kayankaya is our security chief for the next three days, and we all ought to follow his instructions.'

Rashid nodded again. He liked the sound of that: security chief. I was convinced, however, that Katja Lipschitz did not think any greater dangers lay in wait for Rashid than a destitute colleague who might be infuriated by the sight of what went on in luxury hotels to the point of throwing a glass of beer in Rashid's face, or a lady sitting beside him at dinner who struck his hand away from her thigh.

All the same, Maier Verlag should get an author to be taken seriously for the money it was laying out.

I went on. 'In any critical situations, please don't be alarmed. I carry a gun, and will bring it out if necessary. If I have to throw you to the floor or get you into cover in any other way, I'll try to hurt you as little as possible.'

'I see.' He frowned. Either he thought, as I did, that this was a good excuse if the fancy took me to push him into the nearest broom cupboard, or he really did feel a little queasy.

'When you're giving interviews, or you're in contact with your readers, I'll be as inconspicuous as possible, although I must insist that if I feel suspicious – and often that's pure intuition – I shall have the person concerned subjected to a quick search for weapons or explosives. Unless, of course, he or she is well known to you or Frau Lipschitz.'

'Okay...' he said hesitantly.

Perhaps he hadn't imagined my job in such concrete terms, with so much opportunity for hand-to-hand scuffling. Presumably there had been practical, objective reasons for the decision to hire a bodyguard: genuine concern for his safety and the endeavour to make sure he appeared at the Fair to the best possible advantage. However, his image of the bodyguard himself and the nature of his job had probably been more poetic than anything. A mixture of a cheerful companion, Prince Valiant and some Hollywood hero leaping out of a helicopter.

After the barman had brought me my mineral water, Katja Lipschitz asked, 'What line do we take during demonstrations?'

'Demonstrations?'

'Well, there have been indications that there might be protests by Muslim groups at the publishing house's stand.'

'Was that in the threatening letters?' I asked mildly.

'We've had some anonymous phone calls.'

'Well...' I sipped my water. 'Either it's possible to talk to such people, or Herr Rashid and I go off to eat a beef sausage and wait for the demonstration to be over. Are these anonymous phone calls recorded on your answering machine?'

'My secretary took them.'

'You know, there's quite a lot of time between an

anonymous phone call and a face-to-face appearance with a possible police confrontation – time for the caller to consider the tempting idea of staying at home on Day X and lying comfortably on the sofa, putting the next DVD into the slot. Anonymous phone calls aren't often followed up by action.'

'How about cases of explosives?' asked Rashid.

'I assume that visitors to the Book Fair are checked as they come in.'

'Well…' Katja Lipschitz made a vague gesture. 'The checks aren't particularly rigorous.'

'That's a pity. Then we'll have to look out for all bags standing around unattended. And if we' – I gave them a good-humoured smile – 'happen to overlook the one vital bag, then at least we acted in the cause of literature and enlightenment.'

'Yes, well, very nicely put,' said Rashid, while Katja Lipschitz made a face as if I had cracked a joke about blondes.

'But don't worry,' I went on. 'What was it I read the other day? In Europe, the risk of dying in an attack involving explosives is a hundred times less than the risk of choking on a mini-mozzarella. So watch out for the cold buffets over the next few days.'

Rashid tried to make eye contact with Katja Lipschitz. The glance he gave her when she finally looked his way said something like: Can you please get this conversation back on sensible lines at once! Then he took his half-litre cup of coffee and disappeared behind the still-towering foam mountain. Maybe they fixed it with hairspray. If your coffee didn't come with a mountain of foam, Deborah had told me recently, it hardly stood a chance in the coffee trade today. Milky coffee foam had clearly surpassed beer foam as Germany's number one foam. I was wondering if I would think it funny to warn Rashid of the dangers of overfoamed milk when Katja Lipschitz finally brought the pause to an end.

'Herr Kayankaya, I understand that, based on your work

and your experience, you take such a situation less seriously than we do. But please don't forget: Malik is a writer, his world is his desk. The fact that a literary text – and one in which Malik openly pleads for greater tolerance and opposes any form of exclusion or oppression – that such a text, one that sets out to make the world a better and more peaceful place, has led to Malik's having to fear for his physical safety if not, indeed, his life, is a shock that has affected all of us at Maier Verlag, but of course affects Malik in particular and will do so for a long time to come. We would be grateful if you would be a bit more sensitive.'

Before I could nod and say, 'Sorry,' or something of that nature, there was an angry interjection from behind the mound of foam. 'That's nonsense, Katja! I don't want to make the world a better place, if anything I only want to make literature better! You might as well say I wanted to change the world! And there's your nice little UNESCO scribbler! Off I go into the paperback *African Narratives* series!'

Katja Lipschitz froze. I scratched my chin and tried to think of something as sensitive as possible to say. Rashid lowered his cup and shot angry, scornful glances at me. 'As for you, you'd better read my book! Here you are, working for me, and you haven't a clue about it! My novel has nothing to do with your self-indulgent world of mini-mozzarellas!'

'I'm glad to hear that, Herr Rashid. Just now I was afraid, for a moment... well, since you know your way about first-class hotels so well, and if I remember correctly your central character is, well, sexually indeterminate – for a moment I wondered whether the story in your novel is set in the world of flight attendants or interior decorating... if you see what I mean? Something along those lines. But you know,' I went on fast, before he could throw his coffee cup at me, 'I'm just a bodyguard. I never studied at university and I must confess, to my shame, that my reading matter has been confined to the daily TV programmes for far too long. So I'm glad you've given me such a personal incentive to make up for that. I'll read your book as soon as I can, and I really look forward to it. However…'

I stopped. They were both staring at me with their mouths slightly open, as if they were watching acrobatics in a circus. Was I about to break my neck? Would they break it for me?

'Well, since I'll be close to you most of the time over the next few days, I'm wondering whether you wouldn't be uncomfortable if I carried your book around with me? I mean, it's possible that people might get the idea that as your bodyguard I was, so to speak …' I gave a short laugh, 'forced to read it. So, I can simply read it at night. I can get through it by Sunday, and then I'd be delighted to talk to you about it. When does one get the chance to discuss an author's work with the author himself?'

Rashid stared at me for a moment, baffled, then he looked at the black plastic table in front of him and said, in a tone suggesting that he was overcome by exhaustion, 'I have to go to the toilet, and then I think it would be best if we went to the Fair.'

'There's one more thing I'd like to get clear, Herr Rashid.'

Rashid got up from the sofa and asked, turning away from me, 'And that is?'

I noticed Katja Lipschitz's fingers digging into the arms of her chair.

'I appreciate the fact that you address me as a friend, indeed I take it as a great compliment. But over many years I've found that excessive familiarity with the person I am protecting can lead to moments of carelessness in my work. So let's keep it formal until the end of our contract.'

Rashid cast me a quick, expressionless glance over his shoulder. 'Whatever works for you.' And he went off slowly, almost dragging his feet, in the direction of the toilets.

I wondered whether I ought to accompany him, but then decided that my work didn't begin until we were at the Book

Jakob Arjouni

Fair. I thought it most unlikely that Rashid would run into any danger in the toilet.

I sipped some water and turned to Katja Lipschitz. She was still sitting in her chair all tensed up, fingers digging into its arms, eyes turned on the floor.

'Was that sensitive enough?'

She looked up and scrutinised me as if she were asking herself – in as many words, unusual as they might be in her mouth but surely satisfying – what damn whore had brought me into the world? Then she said, 'You know very well that you'd be fired if there was any chance of finding a replacement for you in the next half an hour. What possessed you to speak to our author like that?'

'And what possessed your author to treat me like a fool? "My protector!"'

'It was a sign that he liked you!'

'He doesn't know me at all. Why would he like me? For my origin?'

She took a deep breath. 'Maybe I didn't make it clear enough at our last meeting: Malik Rashid is a great, a fantastic, a very special author, recognised and celebrated all over the world. If at first his behaviour or his style is not easy for you to comprehend, then it may be because you seldom mix with artists and intellectuals.'

I remembered what Valerie de Chavannes had said about her husband: 'Well, maybe your job doesn't allow you much experience with people whose approach to life doesn't conform to the usual standards.' Obviously I didn't exactly strike the ladies of upper-class Frankfurt society as a man of the world.

Katja Lipschitz went on: 'The thought processes of creative minds are often more convoluted and their conduct in public clumsier than ours. Because they think too much!'

God knows no one could say that of you, she said with her eyes.

'Because they try to understand things in all their complexity! And sometimes make them more complicated than they really are. I am sure Malik thought seriously about the way to meet you. Do you know what he said to me on the phone two days ago?'

Being unable to think of anything sensitive, I didn't reply.

'He said how uncomfortable the situation was for him! Giving a grown man instructions about his most intimate affairs. For instance that he'd have to be accompanied to the toilet. Or the other way around, taking instructions from you. The idea that he couldn't go anywhere or do anything he liked. He probably thought it all over carefully – whether a formal or informal approach would relax the situation more.'

'You ought to have suggested that formality is best between adults at the start.'

'Don't be so uppity!'

'You mean that as an Oriental I…'

'Argh!'

'Oh!'

She leaned forward angrily, picked up her coffee, and disappeared, like Rashid, behind a mountain of milky foam.

'Well,' I said, 'I think with that everything's cleared up now.'

Katja Lipschitz was still hidden behind the foam.

'All that remains is for me to wish us all a happy working relationship.' I raised my glass of water. 'Here's to three relatively calm days as uneventful as possible.'

She lowered her cup far enough for us to look into each other's eyes. 'Please just do your work as well as you can. The situation is what it is, and Malik Rashid is Malik Rashid. I'm sure you're professional enough to accept that going forward. If there are any more disagreements or supposed problems, or anything else, please turn straight to me. I'll be the person you talk to for the next three days – and no one else. Malik needs his strength for the fair, and don't even think of approaching members of our staff…'

She was searching for the right word. I helped her out. 'To pester them?'

She took a sip of her coffee. 'You know what I mean.'

'Don't worry. I'll be as invisible as possible.'

'Good, Herr Kayankaya, I'm glad to hear it.'

She put down her mug of cappuccino and said, 'Excuse me, it's the Book Fair and I have things to do.' Then she tapped a text message into her iPhone and checked her emails. Time passed, and Rashid did not come back. I wondered if he suffered from diarrhoea, and imagined the two of us having to go to the toilet together every half an hour for the next few days.

When he finally did come back his temper had greatly improved.

'Right, Herr Kayankaya,' he said in a conciliatory tone. 'Let's do it whatever way you think is right.'

Katja Lipschitz looked relieved.

On the way to the Fair, the mood in our taxi was suddenly really good. Rashid asked Katja Lipschitz who else was coming, maybe Lutz Whosit or 'witty Bodo', how many interviews he was giving, where we could get a quick bite to eat before the evening's event, and he seemed as happy as a child, even if he groaned now and then, 'My God, what a strain this is going to be!'

And to me, he said, 'You wait and see, the Book Fair is hell!' But he was beaming all over his face.

Chapter 11

The Book Fair wasn't hell, it just smelled a bit like it. Huge halls over several storeys, each with a floor area about the size of two football fields, were filled partition after partition with the stands of millions of publishing houses, right to the last corner. A sweating, unwashed, perfumed crowd of humanity, drenched in alcohol, hungover and smeared with hair gel, pushed its way along aisles and past stands, up and down escalators, into toilets and through entrance doors, never stopping. The greasy vapours of sausages, pizza, Chinese food, Thai curry and chips wafted overhead, invisible radiators seemed to be turned up to maximum – or maybe it was just all those bodies producing such heat – and only the few doors opening and closing brought any fresh air into the place.

From Maier Verlag's small hospitality room behind me came the odours of filter coffee stewing on a hotplate, egg and Harz cheese rolls that no one touched and smelled stronger as the day went on, and a homemade coconut and banana cake brought by a young American author for the staff of the firm – *For you guys, for all the amazing work you do!* It seemed to be made of Bounty bars and rotting fruit.

The stand of Maier Verlag was about twenty-five metres

long by five metres wide. Portraits of authors and posters of book jackets hung on the walls, stacks of new releases lay on several shelves. The seating consisted of simple wooden benches and chairs, with small round tables and on each a dish of biscuits and another of salted crackers. A part of the wall some five metres wide in the middle of the stand, as well as a table positioned there with four chairs in front of it, differed from the rest of the furnishings. The wall was adorned with a fishing net, two plastic lobsters, a plastic octopus, a bottle with a letter inside it, a small buoy and five copies of Hans Peter Stullberg's new novel hanging in the net. Its title was *An Occitanian Love*. The table was in the classic French bistro style, with an iron foot and a marble top, the chairs were folding wooden garden chairs in red and yellow. 'The colours of Occitania,' as Katja Lipschitz explained to us.

When we arrived, Rashid had commented dryly on the special presentation of Stullberg's novel with, 'On account of his back trouble.'

There was a whole shelf full of copies of his own novel, *Journey to the End of Days*, with a quotation from *Le Monde* above it. 'Seldom have relevance of content and formal expression achieved such perfect symbiosis.'

'A great quotation,' said Katja Lipschitz.

'Well, *Le Monde* is always *Le Monde*,' agreed Rashid.

And I said, 'Makes you want to read it right away.'

Katja Lipschitz gave me an expressionless look before pointing to the corner next to the hospitality room. 'We thought you could sit there. You'll have a good view of the stand, and you'll be relatively inconspicuous. Malik will be interviewed by journalists and talk to readers and booksellers at the table in front of you.'

'Great,' I said, putting the bag containing my ironed shirt and pin-stripe suit for the evening occasion with Dr Breitel down on the chair intended for me. Rashid pushed his gleaming black rucksack with a little Canadian flag patch sewn onto it and the inscription *Vancouver International Writers' Festival* in red under the table, explained that he was going off for a moment to see people, and began walking round the stand saying hello to the publishing staff; with a hug and a kiss on both cheeks for the women, and a hearty handshake for the men. 'Great book, Malik!' 'Immensely touching!' 'A really important text!' 'My favourite new book this year!'

While Katja Lipschitz turned away to use her phone, I looked around for places where Rashid and I could take cover if need be. In front of us was the aisle with the constant flow of visitors to the Book Fair, to the right the Maier Verlag tables where staff members were discussing sales figures, developments at the Book Fair, personal details, events they were going to attend and the latest Book Fair gossip – 'Gretchen Love!' – 'She's bound to be on the non fiction best-seller list next week!' – 'Crazy!' – 'Scandalous!' To our left there was the partition between Maier Verlag and the neighbouring publisher. On that partition was Rashid's shelf with new copies of his novel, some three hundred of them, the quote from *Le Monde* blown up large, and a photo of Rashid propping his head on three fingers and looking as amused and superior as he had when I walked into the lounge of the Harmonia Hotel.

So the only possible cover was the hospitality room. But by the time we had got the sliding door behind us open and closed again, and flung ourselves down among the trays of rolls and crates of bottled water, any assassin worth his salt would have finished off Rashid with a knife taken from the nearest pizza trolley and disappeared into the throng of visitors again.

Besides my suit for that evening, my bag also contained a baseball bat, pepper spray and a pair of handcuffs. I unzipped it and placed the handle of the baseball bat close to the side of the bag so that I could get at it as quickly as possible. I also took my pistol out of my back holster behind me and put it in the right-hand side pocket of my corduroy jacket. No one could spot the gun there, and I could shoot through the jacket itself.

'I hope you'll be careful with that.' Katja Lipschitz came up to me and pointed to my jacket pocket. 'I've been observing you. I mean, there can also be exuberant fans who might want to embrace Malik.'

'Then that's their bad luck. I rather like firing at random, you know. Right here in the aisle with all the visitors coming to see the show you're bound to hit someone. By the way, do you have those threatening letters with you?'

We looked at each other.

After a pause, Katja asked, 'Do you have a wife, I wonder?'

'You mean am I gay?'

'No, just wondering if anyone lives with you?'

'You'd be surprised: I've been in good hands for more than ten years. We share an apartment, no affairs – at least on my part – which is why I'm so good-tempered, so easy to please, a man surrounded by the warmth of a feminine nest. Sorry about that, in case you were interested in your chances.'

Katja Lipschitz uttered a brief laugh.

'How about those threatening letters?'

'Would the letters change anything in your approach?'

'Yes. I'd know whether I can rely on the information of the lady who hired me.'

Another pause. I heard a cry from one of the other Maier Verlag tables. 'Here, see this text message! Number one!' – 'I don't believe it!' – 'Well, to be honest, I wouldn't mind having someone like Gretchen Love on our list too – you can always sell it as art!' – '*Spermaboarding* as art? I don't know about that.' – 'Is that the title? *Spermaboarding?*' – 'Yes, and something else as well.'

Finally Katja Lipschitz said, 'A few weeks ago Malik said he'd received letters like that. Unfortunately he hasn't brought them yet. I've asked him several times.' She looked at me challengingly. 'Happy now?'

I shrugged my shoulders. 'It's all the same to me what you people do to crank up sales. But it's part of my job to estimate roughly the extent of the danger for the person I am protecting and for myself. I'll assume even more now that we shall have a peaceful afternoon.'

It took her a moment to overcome herself, and then she said, 'Glad you are so relaxed about it. I'm sorry, working with authors' — she hesitated — 'well; they have their oddities, surprises — if you see what I mean?'

'Of course — because they think too much.'

She smiled wearily. 'Then that's all right.' And looked at the time. 'I must get back to the phone now. If you need anything, then as I said, please ask me. See you later.'

Soon after that Rashid sat down at the table in front of me, and Katja Lipschitz's young assistant, wearing a chic blue trouser suit, served him a cup of stewed coffee and a slice of coconut and banana cake.

'Thanks, darling.' He winked at her. 'Mmm, that smells good. Let's hope our young colleague writes as well as he bakes.'

'Oh, he does,' said the assistant with a friendly smile. 'A great book, really moving. If you need anything please ask. The man from the *Bamberger Allgemeine* will be here in five minutes.'

'What about the *Wochenecho* interview?'

'We're still working on it, Herr Rashid. Katja is doing all she can. The problem is that the journalist who agreed to do the interview had to withdraw at short notice for health reasons. I'm really sorry. As soon as there's any news I'll let you know.'

She turned to me. 'Would you like a piece of cake too?'

'No thank you, just a glass of water, please.'

As the assistant went to get the glass of water from the

hospitality room behind me and a cloudy aroma of Harz cheese and banana enveloped me from the open door, Rashid turned to me, glancing at the hospitality room. 'Sweet, isn't she?' Then he held his cake fork aloft like a little sword. 'An interview in the *Wochenecho*! If that comes off then the sales...' And he drew a line slanting up in the air with his fork.

'Great,' I said.

A little later Katja Lipschitz's assistant brought the journalist from the *Bamberger Allgemeine* to Rashid's table. He was a stout, unshaven, uncombed, comfortable-looking man in his mid-forties in trodden-down shoes and a raincoat so crumpled that he might have spent the night in it. He let his apparently heavy shoulder bag drop on the floor and greeted Rashid exuberantly. '...A great honour for me... Very glad to... What a brave book... thank you for giving me your time.'

Rashid tried to return the compliments as far as he could. '...Very glad to meet you myself... thanks for *your* time... *Bamberger Allgemeine*, a great little paper...'

Then the journalist took an old-fashioned tape recorder out of the shoulder bag – 'Afraid we don't run to modern technology at the *Bamberger Allgemeine* yet' – spent five long minutes getting the recorder to work, and finally began asking questions that he had noted down on a small piece of paper covered with food stains.

It was the first interview of Rashid's that I had heard, and there were to be another eight that afternoon: with the *Rüdesheimer Boten*, the *Storlitzer Anzeiger*, the student journal *Randale*, with Radio Norderstedt and someone or other – and little as I liked Rashid myself, by at least the third or fourth interview I was feeling sorry for him all the same.

'My dear Malik Rashid,' went on the man from Bamberg, after a few trivial questions about Rashid's place of birth and biography, 'now let me take the bull by the horns: is your masterly, compelling novel *Journey to the End of Days* not, above all, the subtle coming-out of a man from North Africa who has lived in Europe long enough to throw off the religious and traditional chains of his native land publicly and, so to speak, on behalf of many... how shall I put it? Like-minded men?'

'What?' Rashid's mouth stayed open. He really did seem taken entirely by surprise. He had certainly expected journalists to broach the subject, but he was obviously not prepared for it to be the kernel, not only of this but of all the following interviews on his first day at the Fair. However much he explained that his central character's homosexual love for a young hustler was a mixture of sexual frustration, longing for freedom, the desire for forbidden fruit, with at most a very slight amount of natural inclination, and that he as a writer was simply devising a conflict that would help him to describe the present state of Moroccan society – the one thing that interested the mostly unprepared and cheaply dressed men and women of Bamberg and Storlitz was: DOES THE MUSLIM AUTHOR PUBLICLY ADMIT TO HIS HOMOSEXUALITY?

Just after four o'clock, Sheikh Hakim called me on my mobile. I was standing at the wash basins in the gents' toilet for the third time that afternoon, waiting for Rashid. Maybe it was the scalding coffee that he tipped cup after cup down his throat during the interviews, maybe it was the interviews themselves, but he was suffering from diarrhoea. As I stood next to the room full mainly of men urinating and watched how they carelessly soiled the floor, I gathered from their talk that there were three main topics of conversation at the Book Fair that day. First, Gretchen Love's future best seller *Spermaboarding, or How a Hundred Men Came On Me All at Once*, just published by a large and famous firm, a kind of account of a Berlin porn star's self-exploration. Second, the

Wochenecho journalist Lukas Lewandowski, well known to everyone but me, judging by the general interest and all the laughter, who claimed to have seen a vision of the Virgin Mary in the high-speed train between Hannover and Göttingen on his way to the Book Fair, and thereupon dropped everything worldly, including his work, to devote himself entirely to that experience. Third, a presumably powerful literary critic whose name wasn't mentioned but who was referred to as Blondi a couple of times – whether after the pop band, Hitler's German Shepherd or simply his hair colour was not clear to me – who had published a novel entitled *Oh, My Heart, My Heart, So Heavy Yet So Light* under a pseudonym. That morning his supposedly top-secret pseudonym had been aired in several newspapers, and Blondi had marched up to one of the journalists responsible at the Fair and slapped his face. 'Or more likely spat and scratched the little queen!' said someone in the corner. 'Oh, my heart, my heart, so heavy!' Everyone laughed.

At that moment my mobile rang.

'Good afternoon, my brother.'

'Good afternoon. As far as I know I don't have a brother. Who's speaking?'

'Sheikh Hakim.'

More laughter about something near the urinals.

'Wait a minute, it's rather noisy here.'

I went out into the corridor near the entrance to the toilet.

'Herr Hakim?'

'Kemal Kayankaya,' he stated, pleased. He emphasised the Turkish pronunciation of my name.

'Yes, you have the right number.'

'Not a very Christian name.'

His speech rhythm had the monotony of an electric kitchen machine, and he had a strong accent, but grammatically his German was perfect. His sentences sounded as if he had learnt them with heart – as if speaking German was for him a job to be carried out perfectly, like a dutiful official or a high-class whore, but that hardly interested him at all.

'To me it's just my name.'

He laughed, coughing.

'Why do you fight the fact that you came into the world a Muslim?'

'I don't fight it, but I don't make a big thing of it either. I didn't choose it. Is that why you're calling – for a discussion about the religious traditions of my parents' native land?'

That coughing laugh again.

'My secretary tried to arrange a meeting with you.'

'He told me that you want to see me, and I advised him to fix a time. I'm not often in my office.'

'So I see.'

'You see what?'

'Well, I am sitting in your office at this moment and it really doesn't look as if you spend much time here.'

I took a great deal of trouble to go on in a calm voice. 'Really? Did I forget to lock up?'

That laugh again. It was as mechanical and empty of feeling as his German, and had nothing to do with any kind of amusement.

'Do you know what's interesting?' he asked, without answering my question.

'A great many things in the world, Herr Hakim. But I assume you mean something that I won't think of at once.'

'As far as I can see there's nowhere for you to sleep in your office. Forgive me, but I've never had a chance to see a real private detective's workplace before, and it could have been like the films: that you earn just enough for schnapps and a folding bed behind the desk. And so, at least, I take it that you have a private apartment somewhere. The curious thing is that Methat has searched your office, has looked through all the drawers and files with meticulous care, and he found no address anywhere to confirm my supposition. Do you understand? As if you had calculated on a situation like this and were intent on leaving no traces in your office leading to your private life. Maybe because there is a woman you love in your private life, maybe even children?'

'Herr Hakim, I know that you are active in the field of heavy hints and impenetrable remarks, but I am probably not wrong in assuming that you're not concerned with religion at the moment. If you want to talk about your deplorable nephew, go ahead. If you just want to beat about the bush I'm hanging up. Oh, and kindly get out of my office at once.'

That coughing laugh. Rashid emerged from the toilets beside me, pale-faced. I signalled to him to wait.

'I'd like to put it more plainly but we'd better not do that on the phone.'

'Why not? I have nothing to hide – or, as you would say, I have a clear conscience. How's your conscience, Herr Hakim?'

'Where are you now? I can come to you at once.'

'Sorry, but I'm working. I have no free time until Monday afternoon.'

'I can't wait as long as that.'

I thought of his threat to find out where Deborah and I lived. 'Okay, if Methat tidies up after him and replaces the lock on the door, if it suffered when you broke in, then we can meet late tomorrow evening for a little while in some public place.'

'How about in my mosque?'

'As I understand it, Sheikh, a mosque is more of an intimate place where you talk to the Lord God. I suggest Herbert's Ham Hock at the railway station. If you're hungry they serve salad too.'

He said nothing. I thought I could sense him shaking his head.

Finally he said, suddenly with an icy tone to his voice, 'Don't go too far, Kemal Kayankaya. Very well, tomorrow evening, Herbert's Ham Hock – around eleven?'

'Right at the back of the dining room there's a nook on the left where we can talk undisturbed. I'll have it reserved for us. See you tomorrow evening, then.'

I broke the connection and turned to Rashid. 'Sorry to keep you waiting. How are you?'

'Ah, well…' He sighed. 'I must have caught some bug. Or maybe there was something wrong with the egg salad yesterday evening.'

'If I were you I'd lay off the coffee at the Maier Verlag stand. And the coconut and banana cake, too.'

'I only had a small piece. I mean, a colleague's home-baked cake – you have to try it at least once to be polite.'

'Even if Hans Peter Stullberg had baked it?'

Rashid raised his slightly clouded, sickly eyes from the floor and looked at me. 'He'd have been more likely to heat up some sangria and then do us a dance. Unfortunately his back doesn't allow it.'

I grinned, and we set off back to the Maier Verlag stand.

'Come to think of it,' Rashid said, 'I'm glad that I don't have to take your tone earlier today personally.'

'How do you mean?'

'Well, when you were phoning your client just now you sounded just as grumpy.'

'Hmm. Tell me something: the *Wochenecho*, is Lukas Lewandowski supposed to do the interview?'

'Yes. I heard all that in the toilets as well. The publishing house said it was a "health issue".'

'Well if the story's right, that's what it is, too.'

Just before we reached the Maier Verlag stand, Katja Lipschitz's assistant came towards us. 'Malik! We've been looking for you everywhere. The lady from Radio Norderstedt has been waiting for ten minutes.'

Rashid, still pale from the activity of his intestines, switched in no time at all back to his 'A good thing there are guys like me around' advertising campaign. The colour returned to his face, and his shoulders went back.

'We just went out for a breath of fresh air. Ready in a moment.'

An attractive young redhead with big green eyes, red lips, a short skirt, bare legs and high-heeled boots was waiting at his table. Her lips twitched nervously at regular intervals, making her look vulnerable. You could see Rashid rubbing his hands with glee.

And then the lady from Radio Norderstedt said, after preliminary greetings, 'I'm from the *Other Way Around* programme, and may I tell you how glad I am to have a self-confessed gay Muslim on the programme at last.'

On the way to the House of Literature for the panel discussion with Dr Breitel, I called Deborah from the taxi.

'Everything all right?'

'A full house, I'm busy. Keep it short.'

'Will you wait for me when you close down, please? I'll collect you from the wine bar.'

'Fine. Has something happened?'

'Someone broke into my office, and I don't want you to go home to the apartment by yourself.'

'And there was I thinking it was something romantic.'

'I'll steal you a rose on the way home. See you later.'

The rest of the evening in the House of Literature and the bar of the Frankfurter Hof went, with a few exceptions, that now almost familiar uneventful course that seemed to be the basic tone of the Book Fair. People talked a lot and drank a lot, but what with all the friends, colleagues and acquaintances they were talking to and drinking with, they almost never had time to finish talking to one person on a subject or sometimes even to finish a sentence. As if the room were full of turning circles that only briefly collided with each other, changing direction, bumping into the next circles, and so on and so on.

Unusual event number one: Dr Breitel, who, with his grey flannel plus-fours, leather braces, a bright red-and-blue striped shirt and a yellow bow tie, looked like a cross between a fat Hitler Youth boy and Lady Gaga, talked the usual stuff about 'the threat of an Islamised Europe', yet somehow was taken seriously by almost everyone present as if Kant in person in a grey three-piece suit were speaking on the stage.

Unusual event number two: Gretchen Love entered the main hall of the Frankfurter Hof bar at about eleven, in a close-fitting nun's habit and bright blond Pippi Longstocking braids, and at a rough estimate caused seven hundred male jaws to drop.

Unusual event number three: an intoxicated young colleague of Rashid's, who obviously wanted to make up to Katja Lipschitz, entertained our company for a while with good-humoured gossip about other colleagues and the staff of other publishing firms. As so often that evening, the conversation turned to Lukas Lewandowski, among other things, and the *Wochenecho* interview that had been postponed for the time being. Rashid and Katja Lipschitz agreed for what felt like the hundredth time, with downcast expressions, that this interview might have been/probably would have been/was one hundred per cent certain to have been the starting shot in an unexpected rise in sales of *Journey to the End of Days* and would even have guaranteed the book a place on the best-seller list. The drunken author ruined his chances with Katja Lipschitz with a joke that, for a change, I at least half understood. Rashid, he said, should be glad: Lewandowski's chatter, low in meaningful content but always eloquent, was ultimately a danger to authors. Because his nonsensical sentences sounded so good, many listeners who should have known better let themselves be drawn into one

of his cocaine-inspired ideas. As he saw it, Lewandowski was
the Cristiano Ronaldo of the German culture pages:
incredibly talented 'but not very bright. Well, I ask you: a
vision of the Virgin Mary!'

Maybe it was because Katja Lipschitz didn't understand the
half of that joke that I did understand, namely the bit about
the footballer Ronaldo. Or because she wouldn't allow herself
any doubts about her professional world at midnight and at
an increasingly boisterous party – or so it seemed to strangers
to that world like me – and Lewandowski was clearly one of
the power centres of the book trade. Anyway, she closed ranks
with him surprisingly sharply. 'That's stupid. Lukas
Lewandowski is one of our most important promoters of
literature. I don't like to hear him run down.' A little later the
noticeably less inebriated young author left the party.
However when Rashid and I left the bar of the Frankfurter
Hof, I spotted him in the crowd around Gretchen Love and,
judging by his gestures and the laughing faces around him, he
seemed to be back in form as an entertaining if malicious
humorist.

Apart from that, the circles turned with impressive
regularity. 'Hey, you! It's ages since we met... Absolutely
delighted... I love your interview/dress/contribution to the
debate in the *Berliner Nachrichten*... Oh, there's So-and-So, I
must just have a word with him... back in a minute.'

There was nothing for me to do but smile and shake hands
now and then. Although alcohol during a job as a bodyguard
was strictly taboo on principle, several times that evening I
toyed with the idea of indulging in a small beer. The danger
of an assassination attempt seemed to me as slight as the
likelihood of Rashid's novel reaching the best-seller list
without the headline 'Author Stabbed by Religious Fanatic
in the Frankfurter Hof'.

At one twenty I delivered Rashid by taxi to the Hotel
Harmonia. Ten minutes later Deborah got in, dropped her

handbag on the floor and laid her head on my shoulder.

'Read anything good?' she murmured.

'Read what?'

'Well, isn't there a Book Fair going on?'

Even the taxi driver laughed quietly. As he did so, I noticed a pair of headlights following us in the rearview mirror. On the Bockenheimer Landstrasse, I asked the taxi driver to shake off the car for a twenty-euro tip.

'What's going on?' Deborah was alert at once, lifting her head from my shoulder as we suddenly turned full speed into Mendelssohnstrasse.

'Someone's following us.'

Luckily she was too tired to worry.

We raced round two more corners and jumped a set of red lights, and then we were rid of the car following us.

At home Deborah fell asleep at once on the sofa, while I called Slibulsky.

'Hey, any idea what time it is?' he whispered.

'I'm sorry, but I need your help tomorrow. Urgently.'

'It's not a good time. I have our monthly meeting with the branch managers of my firm at midday tomorrow, and Lara wanted to go to a reading with me tomorrow evening. Don't you know the Book Fair is on?'

'Yes, I know. The Book Fair.'

'Or something like that. Anyway, someone's going to read a bit of his book to us, what's its name, wait a minute... Yes, everything's okay, sweetheart, go back to sleep. It's Kemal calling.' I heard a kiss and some murmuring. Lara didn't particularly like me because I didn't make any effort to take her religious quirks seriously. Slibulsky didn't take them seriously either, but he tried not to show it.

'I'll just go into the kitchen... Right,' he went on, at a normal volume, 'so like I said, he's going to read us a bit of his book. Something philosophical, but straightforward and humorous, Lara says. He looks the way Monty Python would have done a French pop star. Kind of long soft hair, and a blasé face like an ad for aftershave.'

'Lara really seems to like him.'

'She thinks he's super cute and wildly intelligent, and the sight of him makes me feel sick.'

'Well, I don't want to spoil your evening. I'll find someone else.'

'Very funny. I just don't know how I'm going to tell Lara. And if she goes on her own you can bet the philosopher will try to get his claws into her.'

Lara was twenty years younger than Slibulsky, looked like Christina Ricci, and always dressed so that her pretty breasts and behind would show to advantage. I could understand that. What I couldn't understand was why Slibulsky, although she had been living with him for more than four years and as a freelance jewellery designer was more or less living on his money, still seemed to be afraid of losing her at any time and thus missing out on the chance of his lifetime. Although as I saw it, Lara loved him very much, if in her own bitchy way, but that's how she was.

'Maybe Deborah can explain it to her.'

Lara had been in awe of Deborah ever since finding out about Deborah's Jewish grandmother. Once she had turned up at our apartment on a Friday evening with a plaited loaf and candles, intending to celebrate the Sabbath. With the words, 'You go on watching the sports programme, I'm sure this isn't your sort of thing,' she left me sitting on the sofa. It wasn't Deborah's sort of thing either, but for once she went along with Lara's more or less correct ritual just to be friendly, although she said afterwards that from the next week she had to go to a sommelier course on Friday evenings. It was almost true; the course was on Thursdays.

'Explain what to her?' asked Slibulsky.

'That I need you to be with Deborah tomorrow. Someone is out to get me, and I'm afraid he'll try to do it through her.'

'And where will you be?'

'I'm on a bodyguard job all day. Can you have the branch managers meeting at the wine bar?'

'No problem.'

'Okay, then Deborah will call Lara tomorrow morning. And as for the reading, I know an author who'll be reading at the House of Literature next week. His novel is called: *An Occitanian Love*, south of France, lavender fields, older man, young girl, "very movingly told, with a humorous slant, light, without avoiding the big questions in life..."'

'Are you drunk?'

'Just quoting from the ad. I'm working at the Book Fair for a publishing house, and the author, Hans Peter Stullberg, is one of their stars. I'll be meeting him tomorrow, and I'll try to get a personal invitation for you and Lara. I'm sure Lara would like the occasion. It's chic.'

'Older man, young girl... I'm not so sure.'

'Oh, for heaven's sake! What's the matter now?'

'Lara's ex was here the day before yesterday. He's the same age as her, up and coming rock star – you know the kind of thing, clever texts, all that shit – and I felt like my own granny. Hey, don't ash on the carpet, please, and: Assam or Darjeeling tea? Enough to make you sick.'

'Hmm.'

Luckily I heard Lara calling to him at that moment. She didn't like Slibulsky to talk to me for too long.

'Well, fine, then. I'll go back to bed. So Deborah will be calling tomorrow morning?'

'Yes,' I said, and, 'Sleep well,' and we hung up. I recalled how in the old days Slibulsky had been a drug dealer, a bouncer, and even for a while a debt collector and henchman for one of the biggest pimps in Frankfurt. Life was a wonderful thing.

Then I undressed Deborah, put a nightdress on her and carried her to bed.

Chapter 12

In the morning Deborah phoned Slibulsky and Lara, and they agreed that Slibulsky would fetch her from home at ten, go with her to the butcher's and the fishmonger's, then take her to the wine bar and spend the rest of the day there with her. Lara was going to join them in the afternoon when the branch manager meeting was over.

'You can choose any dish you like to make up for missing the reading, kitten,' said Deborah. A little later she said goodbye and hung up.

'What did she ask for?'

'Chicken breast and salad.'

'Wow.'

'Well, it's light, and we don't often get asked for something really light.'

'How about us?'

'I thought you had to work all day?'

'I'll try to drop by later with Rashid. After two days at the Book Fair I need something sensible to eat.'

'Shall I buy ox tongue?'

'I love you!'

When Slibulsky arrived I quickly gave him Valerie de

Chavannes's address and phone number, and asked him to call in for the rest of my fee if he was near there in the next few days.

Then the first thing I did was to drive to my office. As I had expected, the door had been broken down, but otherwise everything seemed more or less in the right place. A mini-book edition of the Koran lay in the middle of my desk, probably some kind of *Best of the Koran*. Inside was a handwritten inscription in German: *For my sadly missed brother. It is never too late for the wisdom of the Prophet.*

I put the little book on the bookshelf, called a joiner to repair the door and then drove to the Harmonia Hotel.

My second day at the Book Fair went more or less like the first. Rashid gave interviews and signed books, I sat behind him in the aromas from the hospitality room – this time there was cold ham and rocket pizza, sausage spread and Camembert rolls – and we went off to the toilets roughly every hour and a half. Rashid's diarrhoea had cleared up, but he drank at least a litre of water per interview. In the evening Herr Thys, the lean, good-looking head of Maier Verlag, aged about fifty-five, gave a dinner in the restaurant of the Frankfurter Hof for authors and the upper echelons of the firm. Thys sat in the middle of the table, with Hans Peter Stullberg on his right, Mercedes García on his left and Rashid at the end of the table between the sales director and Thys's cousin. I sat on my own at the next table, chewing the surprisingly dry saddle of venison in mango and bilberry sauce that the firm had ordered for all the guests.

Thys did not look at all like the usual idea someone who didn't know the book trade would have of a publisher. More like an estate agent or a fat cat banker, with a Prada suit, a chunky watch, hair slightly too long and a little too carefully tousled, and a rather odd, smooth and generally ironic smile that sometimes turned mischievous. He liked to quote Oscar

Wilde, and mentioned his acquaintances among the famous. There was usually 'a good Bordeaux' to drink at such occasions, but first my working day wasn't over yet, and second Deborah and her fresh, fruity wines in the wine bar had weaned me off oak-barrely blended wines once and for all.

'…In Manhattan you have to go to Chelsea in the evening these days, of course. I was there recently with Brandon Subotnik…' Thys paused for a moment and smiled craftily at the company before he went on, pleased with himself. 'His next novel will very probably come out under our imprint…' Thys stopped again, and it was a moment before everyone realised what the new interruption was meant for. Then began a general table-drumming of applause.

After the guest on her left had translated this news for her, Mercedes García cried vivaciously, in English with a strong Spanish accent. 'I love Subotnik!'

'Yes,' said Thys, also in English, '*love* is the right word when it comes to Subotnik! What an amazing author and character! We have been best friends for years and, for example, he never misses sending birthday cards to me, my wife or even my children. With all his success he is still the same kind and attentive person he always was. And what a stylist,' he added, reverting to German, 'what a worker! I'm reminded again of Oscar Wilde. "I was working on the proof of one of my poems all morning, and took out a comma. In the afternoon I put it back again…!"'

General laughter. Hans Peter Stullberg, rather well gone on Bordeaux, growled, 'Wonderful!'

Around ten the company at the table slowly began breaking up. Many of them wanted to go on to other parties, others to a late reading, others again just wanted to reach the bar of the Frankfurter Hof as quickly as possible.

Thys had addressed Rashid only once during the dinner: 'My dear Malik, I'm so sorry – this is a fantastic wine, won't you at least try it?'

'Thanks, Emanuel, but you know my rule: no alcohol.'

'I know, my dear fellow, I know. All the same: cola with venison!'

Otherwise he was either having the new stocking and delivery system explained to him by the sales director, or listening to Thys's cousin as she waxed enthusiastic about Morocco.

'Marrakesh, Agadir, the mountains, the sea, the cliffs – what a beautiful country! And such nice people, and the food! My husband and I have thought of buying a little place somewhere on the coast there.'

Rashid remained taciturn all the time, generally saying just, 'Aha,' or, 'Well, well,' or, 'I see it rather differently,' and as far as I could hear he only once said two consecutive sentences: 'Forgive me, but I've written several novels about Morocco. I'd be glad if you would read the book jacket copy some time.'

'Oh, I know! And I have! All about a homosexual police detective. Great, and such a brave subject!'

So for Rashid the evening so far had been rather unsatisfactory, and I hoped that gave me a chance to keep my date with Sheikh Hakim.

While Thys's cousin joined the small queue of members of the publishing staff that had formed around half the table as Stullberg was leaving, and the sales director was checking the bill, I bent over to Rashid. He was eating a *mousse au chocolat*. Like all the other authors, he was still sitting.

'Can I have a word with you?'

'You're welcome to,' he said, and he probably meant it.

'I have a business meeting at eleven – it won't take more than half an hour. I could fail to turn up, but that would be awkward for me. If you feel like a moment away from the Fair, maybe something small to eat – and it would be excellent – or a fortifying ginger juice or tea to drink, I'd take you to my wife's restaurant. A couple of my friends are there, I'm sure you

151

would like them, and after half an hour I'd be back and take you to the Frankfurter Hof or wherever else you want.'

'Your wife has a restaurant?'

Before I could answer, Katja Lipschitz came over to us and said, 'Sorry, Malik, but Hans Peter is leaving now, and you two won't see each other again tomorrow.'

Rashid half rose from his chair and waved to Stullberg. 'See you soon, Hans Peter! And I hope you feel better!'

'Thanks, Malik. Good luck for your new book. Great reviews! I hope the readers will flock in!'

Rashid sat down again. His mood seemed to have deteriorated even more, if anything. Without looking at me, he said, 'Getting out of here for a moment might be a good idea.'

Just before we left the restaurant, while Rashid was getting his coat from the corner, I asked Katja Lipschitz if she could get me an invitation for two people to Stullberg's reading in the House of Literature.

Surprised, she asked me, 'You like Stullberg's books?'

'Well... please don't say so to Rashid.'

'Of course I won't.' She smiled understandingly.

We drove the first five minutes in silence. I steered my Opel down Kurt-Schumacher-Strasse, past the constable sentry house on the right. No one followed us. Rashid was looking gloomily out of the window. 'I hope the readers will flock in!' The best-selling Stullberg seemed to have finished him off for the evening.

Finally Rashid asked, as if to change the subject, 'What's your wife's name?'

'Deborah.'

'Deborah?' He turned to face me. 'Is she Jewish?'

'Her grandmother was.'

'Didn't that play any part in your marriage?'

'We aren't in fact married. I call her my wife because that's in effect what she is, with or without papers.'

'Aha!' He leaned forward in the passenger seat and grinned at me. He had probably decided that he was damned if Stullberg was going to spoil the evening for him. Rashid suddenly became witty. 'Like the Germans, eh? Married, not married, just so long as…' He winked at me. 'I don't know any other country where so many people live together without being married.'

'What do you mean, *like* the Germans? Want to see my ID?'

'An ID is only a piece of plastic, Herr Kemal Kayankaya.' He paused and waited for my reply. I let him wait.

Finally he changed the subject, but he stuck with ethnology. 'I'm an Arab, yes, but I love the Jews.'

'All of them?'

'Oh, you…!'

I was glad when we arrived outside Deborah's wine bar. He could talk all that nonsense with Lara.

The little bar was full, it smelled of food, it was loud, the waiter was sweating as he carried a pile of plates into the kitchen. Slibulsky, Lara, and Tugba from Mister Happy were there, with Raoul, an old friend and the owner of the Haiti Corner restaurant, Benjamin, another old friend and head of a refugees' advice centre, and Deborah, who was taking a break and eating a slice of ox tongue with potatoes and mayonnaise. I felt like having the same later.

They all seemed rather tipsy, and already in high good humour. They welcomed Rashid, the waiter brought another chair, I gave Deborah a kiss and whispered quietly in her ear, 'I'll be back in half an hour's time. Mind Slibulsky doesn't slap your new guest.'

Deborah glanced at Rashid, who was obviously having difficulty keeping his eyes off Lara's cleavage.

'Back soon.'

In the street I looked again, and this time more thoroughly, for anyone shadowing us. That's to say, I was really looking for Sheikh Hakim's secretary. I was pretty sure it had been Methat following us the evening before. But all I saw was a small delivery van standing in the second row of parked vehicles at the next street corner. An elderly man and a girl sat in the front seat. Father and daughter, I decided.

Finally I got back into the Opel and drove to the station.

Sheikh Hakim was sitting at the table I had reserved. In front of him was a glass of water. He did not have any bodyguards around, or at least I couldn't see them. Maybe they were stretching their legs outside.

At this time of the evening there were few guests left in Herbert's Ham Hock, and most of those still here were quietly drinking their beer. All except for two old men in fine tweed suits, talking and laughing at the tops of their voices as they made inroads into the mountains of meat on their plates and a bottle of schnapps. There were no waiters in sight; they were probably out in the yard, smoking. A cleaning lady had begun wiping the floor, and the smell of the cleaning fluid mingled with the aroma of the specialty of the house. Herbert's Ham Hock had been in existence for more than forty years, and as far as I knew the curtains and cushions had never been changed. Even if the place hadn't been serving grilled or boiled ham hock all day, the restaurant would still have exuded the smell of animal fat from every pore. It was a Nazi joke for me to have invited Sheikh Hakim here.

'Nice place,' he said, after we had greeted one another.

'I knew you'd like it.'

By comparison with the photographs of him that I'd seen on the internet, Sheikh Hakim looked older, thinner, more haggard, greyer – an inconspicuous little man, almost bald, in a black suit. They probably prepared him for photos and public appearances with makeup. I even thought I remembered seeing him with a full, thick head of hair in some younger photographs. Did he wear a toupee in public?

'Thank you for the little holy book.' I took my jacket off and sat down opposite him. He looked at me with a chilly smile. 'I've nearly finished it. Can't wait to find out how the story ends.'

He gave that coughing laugh that I knew from the telephone, and his smile became a little broader but no warmer at all. 'The way it ends is entirely in your hands.'

'The little book?'

He did not reply. At the same moment a waiter came out of the kitchen, saw me and came over to our table.

'A glass of water for me too, please.'

When the waiter left I asked, 'Or did you mean Methat's attempts to follow me?'

Without taking his eyes off me, he reached carefully for his glass and took a small sip before putting it down again equally carefully. He licked his upper lip.

'At any rate, if I get my hands on him he can expect something from me.'

This time his smile was natural. Methat was probably some two metres tall and spent a lot of time in the gym. He must be very strong to have knocked my office door down just like that.

'Herr Kayankaya,' said Hakim finally, 'never mind the talking. I want you to withdraw your statement incriminating my nephew. And I want you to do it tomorrow morning. As I understand from my nephew's lawyers, that will be in your own interest. Your claims concerning what you say took place in my nephew's apartment on that morning are so flimsy that, and I quote the lawyers, you would very probably end up in prison yourself for making a false statement. There is still time to put the whole thing down to momentary confusion, or alternatively, for instance'—he paused briefly – 'to jealousy.'

'Jealousy?'

'Well, the lawyers strongly suspect that you were working

for Frau de Chavannes on the morning in question.'

'De Chavannes? Never heard the name.'

He looked at me expressionlessly, then shrugged his shoulders. 'Never mind, you'll think up some pretext. As we all know, you don't lack for imagination.'

'Thank you.'

The waiter brought my water, and I drank a sip. Hakim was watching me. Maybe he was just putting on a show, but he seemed very sure of himself. Did he have a surprise in store for me? Was there a group of holy warriors waiting round the corner of Herbert's Ham Hock to beat my unbelieving soul out of my body if I refused to withdraw my statement? Or had Methat and his henchmen been sitting in the wine bar like normal guests while we talked here, waiting for Deborah to go outside and smoke a cigarette? Bonk, a blow on the head and off to Praunheim. I suddenly thought of the little delivery van. Suppose the girl was part of this? I'd put her age at fourteen at the most, but admittedly at a distance of ten metres and in the faint light of the streetlamps.

'Do you know what I'd really like to understand? Why are you going to so much trouble for a little bastard like Abakay? I've heard that you improve your cash flow as a preacher by dealing in heroin, and I can well imagine that Abakay is being useful as a smuggler or dealer, but a really important man? You're not so naïve as to trust someone like Abakay.'

His face didn't move a muscle, only his eyes became a little thoughtful.

'And as a cleric... I mean, Abakay sends underage girls out on the street. Is that pleasing in the eyes of the Lord?'

Just then his mobile rang. 'Excuse me.' He took the phone out of his trouser pocket, opened it and said, 'Yes?' Then he said no more for a while, and finally just, 'Very well,' before he closed the mobile and put it down on the table. I was sure that Turkish had been spoken at the other end, and Hakim had replied in German purely for my benefit. I was meant to hear how he conducted short phone conversations in which he was being informed about something or other — a precisely planned operation now in progress?

I realised that my mouth had gone dry, and drank some water. Should I call Deborah? Slibulsky? Ought I to let Hakim see that he was succeeding in frightening me?

Before I could make up my mind, Hakim said, 'First, Erden Abakay is my nephew. Do you have a family, Herr Kayankaya?'

I drank some more water. 'I discovered that I had a half brother yesterday. Probably the result of some little adventure of my father's.'

He didn't even respond with that cross between a cough and a laugh, just twisted his mouth briefly as if at a presumptuous child.

'Second: Erden didn't kill the man, certainly not with a small, sharp instrument neatly driven between the ribs and into the heart. Maybe with a pistol, or he would have knocked his skull in. You know that as well as I do. And it is certainly not pleasing in the eyes of the Lord to pin a murder on an innocent man.'

'Innocent is not the word I'd think of in connection with Abakay. Between ourselves, one of the girls he was offering was twelve at most — that shocks me more than the death of a punter who wanted to abuse a girl like that.'

'How interesting. So you consider your own rules superior to those of the community at large. You know better what is right and what is wrong?' This time there was genuine and slightly malicious satisfaction in his smile. 'Someone like that is known as a fanatic, am I right? I'm sorry, Herr Kayankaya, but we are not talking about morality here. We are talking about established laws and a prison sentence lasting many years.'

'I thought my claims would never stand up in court? Abakay will probably get off with a couple of years.'

'Weak, very weak – that's no way to argue a case. You don't like my nephew, so you want to pin a murder on him, full stop.'

I didn't say anything. There wasn't anything to say. The sheikh was right.

'Furthermore, one can always have the bad luck to encounter a judge whose prejudices weigh more heavily than the facts. I know you would like to forget it, but to many of them we are just Turks.'

'I don't forget it, Sheikh, but I don't base my actions on that principle. Do you know why you have to keep Abakay out of prison?'

'As I said, because he is innocent and he is also my sister's son.'

'No, it's because he's blackmailing you. If you don't get him out of there, he'll send you and your drug deals sky-high.'

His mobile rang again. Hakim held it to his ear, listened for a while, then murmured something in Turkish, closed it and put it in his trouser pocket. Then he leaned towards me over the table, and said quietly, 'Listen to me carefully: the situation has changed. We have a hostage. If you do not withdraw your statement against Erden by tomorrow evening, we shall begin cutting off parts of our hostage's body: toes, fingers, ears and so on. If you tell the police, the hostage will disappear forever. Do you still have my number on your phone from my call yesterday?'

I heard myself replying, in a toneless voice, 'Yes.'

'Good. I shall wait for your call tomorrow. The police are sometimes rather slow. It could be a couple of days before Erden's lawyers hear the news. But I trust you. If you assure me that you have done as I require, we will not injure the hostage, and as soon as Erden is released from custody our hostage will also go free. Do you understand?'

'Yes, I understand. Who…?'

Ignoring my question, he turned away and got to his feet.

After taking a thin, black raincoat off a hook, he came close to the table again, bent forward, looked gravely into my eyes and said, in a quiet but penetrating voice, 'Read the Koran. Learn to forgive a brother like Erden. Learn to forgive yourself. There is nothing bad about being a Muslim, on the contrary. Be proud of yourself. Allah loves those who are happy.' He smiled encouragingly at me. 'I'll expect to hear from you in the morning.'

I watched him go to the door and out into the street. As soon as he was out of sight I snatched my mobile from my bag and tapped in Slibulsky's number with trembling fingers. The first thing I heard was the noise of the bar, then Slibulsky's cheerful voice. 'Hey, when are you joining us?'

'Where's Deborah?'

'Hmm, wait a minute… Behind the bar, opening bottles. Want to speak to her?'

I slumped in my chair with relief. 'No, no, that's all right. Is anyone else at the table missing?'

'No… the superstar author just went out with a girl, probably to feel her up, the horny prick.'

'Oh, shit.'

'Why? I'm glad. He's been hitting on Lara, Deborah, Tugba, and then some girls at the next table, one after the other. Very uncomfortable. He wants to have it off with someone this evening and now he's found that someone. Good for him.'

'Can you please go out and see if he's still around?'

A door opened and closed, the noise of the bar fell silent, then I heard Slibulsky again. 'No, they must be looking for a corner somewhere.'

'Okay. I'll be with you in a minute.'

I put my mobile in my bag and signed to the waiter. 'A double shot, schnapps, please!'

Chapter 13

'I don't know either, she was just suddenly standing at our table. Eighteen or nineteen, I'd say. Done up to the nines – moist lipstick, sexy hippie mini-dress, brightly coloured platform shoes and a book in her hand. By your Monsieur Don't-I-Just-Love-Women.'

'Did he say that?'

'He said a lot of other shit like it.' Slibulsky sighed. 'Particularly when he'd had a drink.'

'An alcoholic drink?'

'Yes,' said Deborah. She was standing behind the bar drying glasses. 'Although he kept on telling us how he never really touches a drop of the stuff. But he could certainly put it back. Almost a whole bottle in half an hour. I bet he binge drinks every few months.'

Tugba cleared her throat. 'And he seems to have loved no end of women. Turkish women, like me. Jewish women, like Deborah. Women who make jewellery, like Lara…'

'But do women who make jewellery love him back?' growled Benjamin, with his eyes half closed. 'When he was asked to shut up for a bit he first looked insulted, then turned to the boutique dolls at the next table. "I just love clothes!"'

Okay, so I'm pretty toasted myself at the moment, but he was much, much worse.'

'Yes, well,' said Slibulsky, returning to the real subject. 'And then Titty-Mouse was suddenly standing in front of him, making out she was a fan of his and asking him to sign her book. Of course he went off like a rocket. To be honest...' Slibulsky cast a quick glance at the bench where Lara had fallen asleep. 'If I'd written a book, and I suddenly had a fan like that standing in front of me – well, I can understand it's a great moment in an author's life.'

'And her shoes alone,' murmured Benjamin, his eyes now tightly closed. 'With those flower stickers all over them – wow!'

'Can we have our bill, please?' called a man in the corner. He and the woman with him were the last guests in the bar.

An hour later Deborah and I were lying in bed. While I told her about the day's events in rough outline, her eyes were closing, and by the time I'd finished I was sure she was asleep. But suddenly she said, with her eyes closed and her voice husky with wine, 'What possessed you to pin the murder on him?'

And all of a sudden I had Sheikh Hakim in bed beside me.

I thought again about the moment when I'd got to work on Abakay's chest with the knife. And of how I hadn't just left it at assumptions when I was talking to Octavian, I'd claimed there was no alternative to Abakay as the murderer.

Finally I explained, 'There was a sixteen-year-old girl in that barred and soundproofed room. She was shaking all over. She'd put her finger down her throat and smeared herself with her own vomit to keep a fat drunk from raping her. I'd rather not know how many girls' lives Abakay has ruined like that, and I thought he never ought to get the chance to do it again.'

For a while Deborah didn't react. Then she opened her

161

eyes, turned to me and put a pillow under her head.

'I hope you remember who you're sharing your bed with? That's the kind of thing that happens to tarts. Not all of them, but a great many. I was lucky, but I knew some girls who weren't. And you yourself, you've only forgotten it. Today what happened to your client's daughter seems to you like the worst of nightmares, but back then – don't you remember how we would sit in some bar at five in the morning, finished, broke, drunk – just hoping for another customer, or not to get AIDS, or to find some fool ready to pay for a round of drinks? You, me, Tugba, Slibulsky, all the others. Some dead and buried long ago, others living in the West End. You've grown old, darling, old and soft, and that's just fine – but you'll call Octavian tomorrow and withdraw that stupid statement.'

I said nothing. I imagined Abakay's sense of triumph.

'Do you have any idea who the real murderer might be?'

Would he dare to turn up at the de Chavannes villa again?

'I asked you a question.'

'I don't know,' I replied absentmindedly.

'Oh, come on, darling.' She dug a finger into my stomach. 'You're only a little bit old and a little bit soft, and what's more, you only live in the West End because of your ambitious girlfriend. Could you please put the light out now?'

Next morning I rang Octavian. It was Sunday, and he was having breakfast with some Romanian relatives.

'What did you say?'

'I said I'm withdrawing parts of my testimony. When I got into Abakay's apartment I supposed, wrongly, that Abakay had killed Rönnthaler. Unfortunately I didn't leave Abakay time to explain himself, but believing that I was in acute, life-threatening danger I overpowered him at once. Well, you know the rest – I tied him up and gagged him.'

'You did... And how about the cuts on Abakay's chest?'

'No idea.'

There was a pause. I could hear Deborah squeezing oranges in the kitchen. Octavian's agitated breathing came over the phone.

'You realise this means we'll have to let Abakay go free?'

'He's still a pimp and a drug dealer. It's just that you don't have me as a witness anymore.'

'Oh, nonsense! Kayankaya, you really are such an idiot! How do I look now?'

'Good luck, Octavian. That's all I can say.'

'Wait a minute! This will have consequences. People will make life hard for you, and it wouldn't surprise me if you lose your licence.'

'People? Or you?'

'You can at least be sure I won't lift a finger for you again!'

'That's a pity, when I was hoping for your support, my friend.'

'Arse-hole!'

We hung up, and I called Sheikh Hakim.

'I've withdrawn my statement.'

'Excellent, Herr Kayankaya. The rest will be as we agreed.'

'How's the hostage?'

'The hostage wants for nothing, don't worry. You'll be hearing from me. God be with you.'

For a change, I hoped so too.

At eleven I was supposed to be at the Book Fair with Rashid. According to his schedule, he was reading at eleven thirty with Ilona Lohs on the subject of losing your native land, under the heading 'Sweet Homeland, Sore Hearts.' According to the flyer for the reading, Ilona Lohs was born in the GDR, and her novel *Moon Child*, about eighteen-year-old Jenny Türmerin who wants to flee former East Germany, was based on autobiographical experiences. Malik Rashid – also according to the flyer – missed 'the old, multi-cultural

Morocco where Muslims, Christians and Jews lived side by side,' and in his new novel *Journey to the End of Days* he described, 'among other things, the consequences of increasing ethnic uniformity: the dumbing down and brutalisation of Moroccan society as a whole and the loss of imagination and dreams.'

I was nervous when I called Katja Lipschitz.

'Good morning, Herr Kayankaya. Everything all right?'

In the background I heard what was now, even for me, the familiar roar of the Book Fair. All the sounds in the huge hall mingling into a single, metre-high, continuously rolling ocean wave.

'I can't call it that. Rashid has been abducted.'

'What?!'

'There obviously *was* something to those threatening letters and phone calls.'

'Phone calls?' She raised her voice. 'There weren't any phone calls! I was only saying so! And as for the letters... Oh, nonsense! For God's sake! Are you sure he hasn't simply gone off somewhere, met a woman, oh, I don't know what...?!'

'I'm sorry. The kidnappers called me.'

'What are they asking?'

'Nothing so far. But they told me the name of their group: The Ten Plagues.'

'But... but that's the exact title of Dr Breitel's speech!'

'Well, maybe they read the *Berliner Nachrichten*, or Breitel found the name on the internet in the course of his research.'

'I can't understand it, Herr Kayankaya! Not in my wildest dreams did I think that Malik would really... oh, poor man! I'm so sorry.'

'You must keep calm now, Frau Lipschitz. Say that Rashid is sick, a bad sore throat or something like that. And whatever you do don't call the police! I'll do all I can to get him out of there as soon as possible.'

'But I must tell our publisher. What will happen if they

demand money? Or if they want us to pulp Rashid's novel? Like the Rushdie case, do you remember?'

'Wait before speaking to your publisher. I didn't get the impression that the kidnappers were after money. They're probably more interested in setting an example: see how we can scare you in the middle of your own country. A demonstration of power, if you see what I mean? Or to satisfy their vanity – with terrorists that's usually the main motive. Maybe it can be settled with a simple press release giving the name of the group.'

'I hope with all my heart that you're right. But what am I to do now?'

'As I said, announce that Rashid is sick and say no more. I'll call you the moment I have any news.'

'Do you know what? It's those supposed men of God! I'll pray for Rashid!'

'That's a good idea, Frau Lipschitz. You can't do anything better. See you soon.'

Chapter 14

Abakay was released from custody on Wednesday. On Thursday I had a phone call from someone who worked for Sheikh Hakim.

'Do you know the café in the little tower up in the Grüneburg Park, opposite the Korean Garden?'

'Yes.'

'You can pick up your man there this evening at ten.'

At nine thirty I was going along the path to the tower, among trees and shrubs. There was no one about in the light drizzle in the Grüneburg Park at this time of day. Once I smelled cigarette smoke, probably from someone sleeping rough under the bushes somewhere.

The little tower was dark, and dim light came only from the narrow street about fifteen metres away. Where there were café tables and chairs on the gravel during the day, only a solitary garbage bin covered with advertising for Langnese ice cream now stood in the gloomy night. I had two pistols with me: my official one, registered and in a back holster, and an unofficial, unregistered one – at least, not registered in my name – that I had picked up a couple of years before while searching the apartment of a crack-dealing banker.

I leaned against the little tower for a while, watching the forecourt in front of it, the bushes round it, the street and the entrance to the Korean Garden. Nothing was moving, and after a while I went over to the garbage bin and put the loaded gun that wasn't registered in my name down under it. Just in case, and supposing God wasn't with me after all.

For a moment I had thought of asking Slibulsky to come with me to cover my back if necessary. But for one thing I didn't want to hear Lara bitching about it, and for another I didn't think Sheikh Hakim would cheat on the deal. After all, so far as I could judge, he was not a cleric but a professional gangster. There was really only one possibility that worried me: that of Abakay bent on revenge.

'…Kemal, you motherfucker! Come on out, you tramp! You bloody little sod! Come and get your shitty poet… Hey there!'

I assumed it was the same white delivery van that had been standing outside the wine bar on Saturday evening. Barely two minutes ago, Abakay had driven it with verve over the pavement and into the gravel forecourt. Now he was striding up and down with large, angry, slightly unsteady footsteps, hectically smoking a cigarette held in his left hand and shouting into the night. His right hand was in the side pocket of his leather jacket, and he was taking no trouble to conceal the fact that he was holding a pistol; the shape of the barrel stood out clearly.

'…Where are you, Kemal? Got no balls, you cowardly bastard? Don't you want your crybaby writer back anymore?'

I waited to see if anyone else got out of the van, but apparently Abakay wanted to settle accounts with me on his own. Rashid, I assumed, was tied and gagged in the back of the van.

Presumably he'd snorted a good amount of cocaine to get

167

him into this belligerent mood. In a football match you'd have described him as over-motivated.

Finally I came out from the shadow of the little tower. My own right hand was also on the pistol in my jacket pocket.

'Hello, Abakay. Those elegant expressions... anyone could tell at once that we have a fine, socially committed mind here. How's the photography going?'

He stopped short, then with his jaw wide open and a dismissive gesture of his hand, exclaimed, 'There you are, you pisser!'

'Where's Rashid?'

'Where do you think? In the back of the van. So scared he's shitting himself. What a stench!'

We were standing about ten metres apart. Abakay tossed his cigarette end into the gravel, swaying as he did so, and shouted, 'Totally disgusting!' and sniffed noisily. He seemed to be in a bad way; he had probably had a lot to drink with the coke, and I made the mistake of thinking I was both mentally and physically superior to him just because I was sober. Not even the pistol in his jacket really scared me. The barrel was pointing all over the place, but not at me. Abakay looked as if he might collapse at any moment.

It had been way too long since I'd been in a cheap dive. Every second brawl in a bar followed the same pattern: the guy who was falling-about drunk almost toppled off his bar stool, someone said, 'Come on, old boy, you've had enough.' And then suddenly the drunk could do things with that bar stool... hit the nearest man over the head with it, for instance, or fling it into the shelf of bottles behind the bar. And then four or five men would throw themselves at him all at once, only to find that they couldn't control the drunk in his unbounded rage.

That was exactly what happened to me. I had forgotten that quantities of coke and alcohol didn't make a man incapable of such an explosion. And Abakay exploded! All of a sudden he came at me with wild, long strides, screaming. He suddenly snatched the pistol from his jacket and fired it into the air, and before I could even move my own gun in his direction the butt of his smashed into the middle of my face. I fell backwards, feeling the blood spurt from my nose. At the same moment Abakay first kicked the pistol out of my hand with his black cowboy boots, and then, with two neat dance steps, took a run-up and kicked me twice in the belly with all his might. I threw up.

'Hey there, Kayankaya, you fuck-face! Not as fast as you used to be, right? Know what I'm going to do now? Work you over the way you worked me over – that's fair, right? No more and no less. Know what my chest looks like? Like some shitty geometrical drawing!'

I lay writhing in the gravel, and could look up just far enough to see the knife that he drew out of his boot.

'No!' I wanted to scream, but it was only a gurgle.

'No? What do you mean no, you wanker?' This time he kicked me lower down, and I simultaneously screamed and pissed myself.

'Well, well, well, didn't you know? Always better to go to the toilet before you leave the house. And that's nothing yet – do you know my balls are still swollen? The hospital doctor fears there'll be permanent damage… hear that? Permanent damage! And your doctor will say so too – you can piss your pants full again to that!'

'Abakay… let it…'

'Well, if you say so. Right, I'll just go home…'

He laughed. Then he bent down and held his knife in front of my nose. 'My geometrical pen…'

This time I intended to gurgle and sound as pitiable as I could. 'No, please… stop it…'

At the same time I was crawling away from Abakay. It was meant to look like an act of pure despair. I hadn't the faintest chance of getting away. As soon as Abakay liked he could simply plant his boot on my neck, or shoot me in the legs, or anything else. And confident in that sense of absolute power he looked at me, grinning, as I neared the garbage bin on all fours, with vomit dripping from my chin.

'Very brave! Know what I'm thinking of as I see you arse-up like that? Which would leave more permanent damage, a kick in the arse from behind with the toe of my boot drawn up, or from in front with my heel going right into your soft parts...?'

'Abakay, let it alone... believe me, you don't have a chance...'

'What was that?'

I crawled on, on and on.

'Go home, that's best...'

'You're an odd one, eh? Shall I tell you something? Sure, I'll go home — just as soon as your balls are kicked to mush. Right, that's enough talk...'

I was still about half a metre from the garbage bin when he kicked me in the stomach again. Another gush of vomit, and then everything went black before my eyes.

When I came back to my senses, Abakay was sitting astride me, cutting open my shirt and T-shirt.

'Ah, good morning... Here we go. I thought we'd start with building blocks, go on to circles and end with some nice straight lines — they're sure to look pretty.'

'Let it go...' I whispered. 'Please...' And at that moment I was asking as much for my own sake as his. But of course he didn't understand that.

He mimicked me. 'Please, please, please! Dear Erden, I treated you like dirt, but please, please don't hurt me now!'

He was holding my arms down on the ground with his knees, the way children do fighting in the school yard. My right hand was still about half a metre from the garbage bin.

'Right,' he cried finally, when my chest lay bare before him and I was breathing heavily, and he swung his knife in the air like a magic wand. 'Watch out, or it may go into your eye!'

He was still laughing when I reared up strongly and threw him over to one side. He landed in the gravel, knife raised, and went on laughing. 'A bit of action at last!' He could still easily have stabbed me. He watched me turn and crawl on.

'So where do you think you're going?' With an amused expression, he propped his elbow in the gravel and leaned his head on his hand. 'Throwing yourself away in the garbage?'

I managed to grasp the pistol hidden in the shadows. I'd have liked to go on lying there. Every fibre of my body longed to sleep for a moment in the soft, warm, comfortable gravel.

'And now, arsehole?'

'Now no more geometry,' I whispered as I turned round and shot him first in the face and then, to make quite sure, in the chest.

It took me about twenty minutes to get to my feet. I put my pistol away, staggered over to the little tower, picked up the second pistol and stood there breathing heavily. For a while I looked at the gloomy scene: Abakay, the drizzling rain, the garbage bin, the Langnese advertising cardboard. I'd had no choice. In his mood just now, Abakay wouldn't have stopped short at slitting my chest open and kicking me between the legs. One way or another, he'd have crippled me.

Finally I pulled myself together and staggered over to the delivery van.

The key was in the ignition. I could hear Rashid kicking the bodywork of the van from inside. I started the engine, and Rashid howled. They must have promised him his freedom and now he thought something had gone wrong.

Cautiously, I drove down the street and through the West End, then past the old opera house and to the Frankfurter Hof. I parked the delivery van in a nearby side street, wiped my fingerprints off the steering wheel and the knob of the gear lever, got out and opened the door to the boot. In fact, Rashid stank even worse than I did. He was wrapped in sticky tape like a mummy, with only his nostrils free. With the help of my pocketknife I removed the tape from his ears first.

'Don't worry. It's me, Kayankaya. You're safe now.'

He tried to say something. With a jerk, I tore the tape off his mouth. Bits of skin and stubble came off with it, and blood seeped through his cheeks in several places. He groaned with pain and began shedding tears.

'Thank you...'

'I'm sorry, I must leave your eyes taped up for a moment. For your own safety. You don't need to see the car we came here in. It's the kidnappers' vehicle, and the less you know the better.'

The better for me too.

Then I began unwrapping his body. At first he could move his arms and legs only with difficulty. After that I led him down the street to a driveway, where I carefully removed the tape from his eyes.

He blinked. 'Oh, my God!' and looked round in confusion. Then a smile spread over his face, suddenly he laughed out loud, flung his arms round me, kissed me on both cheeks and cried, 'Thank you, many, many thanks! It was hell! Those bastards!'

He hugged me. When he let me go, he was still smiling, but he also looked slightly unsure of himself. 'Excuse me, but – do you stink like that or is it me?'

'I think we both need a shower. One of the kidnappers kicked me in the belly a couple of times for fun.'

'And hit you in the face – it looks all swollen.'

'Hmm-hmm. How did they treat you?'

'Oh...' He shrugged his shoulders. 'Well, they didn't mistreat me, at least not physically. Except for hitting me over the head outside your wife's restaurant. I had enough to eat and drink, a bed, a TV set. However... their faces were covered up, and when they said anything it was in Turkish, and however often I told them I didn't understand their bloody lang – oh, sorry!'

'No problem.'

'And then the prayers. They kept coming into my room to pray, and made me pray too. Once, when I refused, at pistol point – oh, it was horrible! However... well, I never felt it was really about religion. Do you understand? I mean, about some kind of religious re-education. Of course that was my first thought, because of the novel. But then... in all those five days no one talked to me about my work. Or not in any language I could understand. But I suppose that's why they kidnapped me...' He seemed to be thinking, and then he shook his head and said, in a loud and contemptuous voice, 'Such arseholes!'

I clapped him on the shoulder. 'Well, you made it. I told Frau Lipschitz this morning that if all went well, you'd be free this evening. She's booked you a room in the Frankfurter Hof, and she's waiting for us there with your publisher. It's just round the corner. Shall we go?'

He looked a bit surprised. 'That's nice of them.'

On the way I said, 'And in the hotel we'll have to discuss the text being released to the press.'

'What text?'

'It was the condition for freeing you. The group that kidnapped you wants, first and foremost, for the world to know that they exist. They call themselves the Ten Plagues.'

'What? Like Breitel?'

'Yes, well.'

'Imagine that! And I was sure he'd just made the whole thing up!' He thought about it. 'But now I'm free... I mean, why would we go along with what the kidnappers want?'

'Think about it.'

He did, and we walked on side by side in silence.

Just before the entrance to the Frankfurter Hof, he said, 'You know what I don't understand? The girl, the decoy – how does a strictly religious group come by a super-Lolita like that?'

'Well, they probably hired her.'

'You mean she was a whore?'

I nodded.

'A whore! Damn it all… I write about that milieu but, to be honest, I just hate…'

'Careful,' I interrupted him. 'No need to insult my wife.'

'What? How do you…'

We reached the steps up to the entrance. Two uniformed pageboys inspected us, horrified: two men with filthy trousers, stinking of vomit, one with cheeks torn and bleeding, the other with a swollen nose.

'Good evening,' I said. 'We're expected. Maier Verlag, Emanuel Thys.'

Chapter 15

I spent the following week waiting. For the police, for Hakim's people, for anyone who put two and two together and thought: if Abakay found himself in jail because of a false statement made by Kayankaya, then presumably he wanted revenge, and presumably Kayankaya would defend himself – so let's ask him where he was on Thursday evening. But obviously no one wanted to put two and two together. The police were glad that arresting Abakay did not, in retrospect, seem such an unfounded notion – the newspapers and the local TV soon agreed that he had died in the course of a drug deal. And Hakim was rid of a troublesome accomplice and blackmailer – family or not.

In the end, I suppose too many people profited by Abakay's death for there to be any serious investigations. And where the police were concerned, that also seemed to close the Rönnthaler case for the time being. By now, at police headquarters, they were probably laying the blame on Abakay after all. If only for a better rate of cases solved.

On Saturday several newspapers printed the press release from Maier Verlag, along with comments and leading articles: *Malik Rashid, author of the novel* Journey to the End of Days, *has been released unharmed after his five-day abduction by a group calling itself the Ten Plagues. The group justified its actions by charging that Rashid's novel insulted people of the Muslim faith. The Ten Plagues wanted to send out a signal. The author's abduction ended, without bloodshed, on Thursday evening.*

One comment pointed out: *However, there is food for thought in the name of the group. Is it just a coincidental prank, or was there a clever mind behind it? Are we dealing with a Muslim combat group whose members read the works of Dr Breitel? That would explain why the abduction went comparatively smoothly: it involved intellectual young men, devout Muslims, probably students, who wanted to distinguish themselves from the image of the primitive bin Laden disciples who murder indiscriminately. Are we facing a cross between guerrilla warfare for fun and serious discourse?*

And so on. The Ten Plagues were initially featured in the news sections of the papers, then the comments, and almost all the papers published interviews with Rashid.

On Monday Slibulsky dropped in and brought me the money from Valerie de Chavannes.

'Wow, what a lady!'

'Hmm-hmm.'

'I'm to tell you that she very much wants to see you.'

'Is her husband back?'

'No idea. Kind of a big black man?'

'Big, I don't know.'

'He passed me in the hall, but we weren't introduced.'

'Thanks, Slibulsky.'

'Tell me,' he said, looking at me curiously, 'is there something going on between you two?'

'Am I crazy?'

'I should think she could drive a man crazy.'

On Tuesday Octavian called.

'You've probably heard or read that your friend Abakay was shot shortly after his release from custody.'

'Saw it on *Hessen Nightly*.'

'Ah – I didn't know it was on *Hessen Nightly*…'

'Would you have wanted to see it too?'

He sighed. 'Listen: there was very probably a fight between Abakay and his killer before the fatal shots were fired. There was vomit all over the dead man, and it wasn't Abakay's.'

'Oh? How interesting.'

'Well, my colleagues are more or less agreed that Abakay got what was coming to him on account of quarrels of some kind on the drugs scene, and there's a lot to suggest that they're right. But out of pure curiosity I asked for a list of the components of the vomit.'

'Oh yes?' I began to sweat slightly.

'And then I called the wine bar and asked what was the dish of the day last Thursday. It was goat ragout with white beans.'

I said nothing. There wasn't anything to say.

'Well, I just wanted to advise you not to attract any attention in the city for a while. Best if my colleagues forget you exist.'

There was a pause. It cost me an effort, but I said, 'Thanks, Octavian.'

When we had hung up, I went into the kitchen and drank a schnapps.

On Friday I went to see Edgar Hasselbaink.

Chapter 16

It was just after seven in the evening when I rang the bell at the garden gate. Warm yellow light shone from the windows of the de Chavannes villa and a faint aroma of fried onions wafted through the front garden.

It was a few minutes before the housekeeper, wearing a white apron, opened the front door, took a brief look at me, and then pressed a button that made the garden gate swing open.

'Good evening,' I wished her once I was inside.

'Good evening,' she replied without a trace of friendliness. 'Who shall I say it is?'

I smiled at her. 'Nice to see you again. Kayankaya is the name. I was first here two and a half weeks ago and since then there's been one question I can't get out of my head.'

'I'm busy cooking supper.'

'As I said, just one question. I'm sure you can remember the day of my visit. It was the Wednesday when Marieke came home.'

She raised her eyebrows disparagingly. 'How often do you think she comes home?'

'You mean how often does she go missing?'

'The supper, Herr...'

'Kayankaya. This won't take long. That morning two and a half weeks ago – why were you so surprised that I was still here when you saw me leaving?'

She stopped, frowned, looked reluctant to reply. 'Why would I be surprised?'

'Because you had heard the front door open and close once already. And you thought there was no one in the house but me and Frau de Chavannes...'

'Well, I'm sorry, but I don't remember either that morning or you yourself, even if that may seem unlikely to you...' A slightly malicious smile hovered briefly on her lips. 'So many people go in and out of this house.'

'You mean it's not like the old days, when the de Chavannes parents kept a calm, decent household.'

'I don't mean anything.'

'Fine,' I concluded. 'Then would you please tell Herr Hasselbaink that I'd like to see him?'

At the same moment the living room door opened and Valerie de Chavannes came out into the hall. She stopped in surprise, and you couldn't describe it any other way: her face was radiant with delight. She cast a quick glance back into the living room, where the TV was on, closed the door and came towards us.

'Herr Kayankaya!' she said, just loud enough to be heard only in the hall. She was wearing a lightweight, red summer dress that flowed down her firm body, which showed distinctly through the flimsy material. She was barefoot. Without taking her eyes off me she said, 'That's all right, Aneta, I'll look after Herr Kayankaya myself.'

The housekeeper looked briefly from Valerie de Chavannes to me and back again. 'Supper's nearly ready,' she said, and disappeared into the kitchen.

Valerie de Chavannes came close to me, looked into my eyes and said in a low voice, almost a whisper, 'Hello.'

'Hello, Frau de Chavannes. I'm really here to see your...'

She laid her fingertips on my mouth and said a quiet, 'Ssh,' as if soothing a child. Then she took my arm and led me into the front garden.

'Are we going for a walk?' I asked.

She didn't reply, just laughed briefly and quietly. Was she drunk? But she didn't smell of alcohol. Other drugs?

In the shadow of a bush, she took my head in both hands, looked deeply into my eyes again and drew my mouth close to her full, dark lips. It was a fervent, moist kiss, as soft as it was determined; I felt the light play of the tip of her tongue, and I had to pull myself together not to attack her.

When she ended the kiss, her hands slid down my hips and she said, sighing, 'I knew it. I knew that very first time that you would help me.'

She said that very formally. I'd once read that upper-class French people, even when they're married, quite often address each other formally. When I read that I thought it crazy. Kissing, in bed, after making love? Now I realised that the idea appealed to me.

'I'm so grateful to you.' She let her hands slip a little further down. 'You're wonderful. I... if I can ever do anything for you...'

Anything – good heavens.

'Forgive me, Frau de Chavannes, this is all delightful, but what are you talking about? I brought your daughter home quite a while ago.'

She looked at me, wide-eyed. 'About Abakay, of course.' Her voice was unsteady. 'You did it for me, didn't you?'

It took me a moment to let that remark, with all its implications, sink into my mind, and then I suddenly had to laugh. I listened to myself: a dry, incredulous, harsh laugh. In fact I was afraid. What a twist that would have been: to think that I might be convicted after all of Abakay's murder in this roundabout way!

'I hope you haven't mentioned this utterly crazy idea to any of your girlfriends, maybe at the tennis club?'

'What…?' Her radiant smile, so seductive and promising a moment ago, was gone, and she looked genuinely taken aback. She retreated a step. 'What do you mean?'

'I mean you must be rather lonely to think up something so outlandish.'

'What do you mean, outlandish? I read it in the paper, and after all that there's been between us…'

'All?' It was hard to believe, but nothing suggested that she didn't mean it seriously. 'We flirted a little, that's all, Frau de Chavannes.'

'Flirted,' she repeated incredulously.

'Yes, that's what it's called. I didn't want either to marry you or to run off to South America with you.'

I looked from the bushes to the villa, and the fence between the garden and the road. 'Is this your secret place for seeing special visitors?' And when she didn't answer: 'Did you meet Abakay here? Arrange to look at photos back at his place?'

'You…! Shut up!'

I nodded. 'Okay. If you'll promise me not to spread any romantic fairy tales about us. Abakay was shot in connection with his drug dealing. You can be glad about that if you like. And now I would like to speak to your husband.'

She looked irritated. 'My husband?' And then, suddenly sounding anxious, 'What do you want to do that for?'

'A friend of mine has a gallery and would like to meet him.'

'So you came here specially for that?'

'I happened to be in the neighbourhood.'

She stared at me. All of a sudden she looked very tired, thin and positively unhealthy. She had folded her arms and was standing in a slightly stooped position, all the tension drained out of her body.

'You needn't show me in, I can find the way myself. If you'd like to think for a little…'

She hesitated, and then said contemptuously, 'Yes, I would like to reflect for a little.'

I raised my hand in farewell. 'Good luck, Frau de Chavannes.'

She didn't move. She was looking at the ground, as if she were inspecting her pretty bare feet in the grass. Those pretty feet and legs, in fact everything about her… it was a shame. I turned once more at the front door. Valerie de Chavannes was still standing in the shadow of the bushes. A passerby might have taken her for a statue.

In the hall, I heard the sound of a mixer in the kitchen, and the TV was on at high volume in the living room. I hammered on the living room door with my fist.

'Yes?'

I went in and saw Edgar Hasselbaink lying on the grey cord sofa that was as big as my living room. He wore a lemon-yellow, close-fitting linen suit, bright blue sneakers, and his curly hair, which was about twenty centimetres long, stood out wildly in all directions. Under the suit jacket his chest was bare, and his dark, muscular, obviously very fit torso was on view. At first sight he looked like a mixture of a crazy professor, a hipster and a model for summer fashions.

I imagined Valerie de Chavannes beside him in her thin red dress, and wondered what they were playing at. Saint-Tropez in autumnal Frankfurt? Or did they dress up in the evening just to look sexy for each other? And then did they watch the news together? And eat supper afterwards?

'Good evening, Herr Hasselbaink.'

'Good evening.' He turned his head to me, but otherwise stayed comfortably outstretched. He pressed the remote control in his right hand and muted the voice of the news presenter on the TV.

I glanced briefly through the door into the hall. 'Where's your daughter?'

'My daughter?' He slowly sat up. 'Probably up in her room. Why?' He spoke with a slight Dutch accent.

'My name is Kayankaya, and I am a private detective.' I was watching his face closely. 'We don't know each other, but perhaps you have seen me before, or at any rate heard of me.'

Nothing gave away what he was thinking; he just looked irritated. 'What are you talking about?'

'May I have a private word with you somewhere we can't be disturbed?'

He kept his eyes on me, looking thoughtful and increasingly anxious.

'Yes, of course.' He got up from the sofa and automatically did up one button of his jacket. A bare chest didn't suit the situation. 'In my studio.'

He walked past me and out into the hall. He was a good head taller than me, an impressive figure.

The studio was in the basement, and there were only two small skylights to let in natural light. Edgar Hasselbaink pressed the light switch, and four white, bright neon tubes came on.

'I always thought that light was all-important for painting,' I said.

'Well, don't I have light in here?'

'I meant natural light.'

'It depends what you're doing. I don't paint trees in the sunset, if you see what I mean.'

'I think so.' I looked at the picture standing on an easel in the middle of the room. It was probably what he was working on at present. A sleeping girl against a blue background, presumably Marieke.

Hasselbaink followed my glance. 'My daughter. There's no more beautiful sight in the world than your own child sleeping peacefully.'

183

'Hmm-hmm.'

'Do you have children?'

I shook my head. 'On the other hand, I can imagine few things in the world worse than seeing your own child unable to sleep for fear, don't you agree?'

Hasselbaink had propped himself on a table in the corner and started rolling a cigarette. 'Yes, I do.' He rolled up the paper. 'And now? What do you want?'

'Your wife mentioned that you studied medicine in Amsterdam before you began your career as an artist.'

He stopped rolling the cigarette and looked up. 'Yes, for two years. Because my parents insisted on it. Why?'

'It must take a certain knowledge of human anatomy to be able to stick a shashlik skewer into a man's chest so that it passes between the ribs and into the heart. The study of medicine is one way of acquiring such knowledge.'

Hasselbaink looked at me, his mouth slightly open, the almost-finished cigarette between his fingers. He looked very calm, thoughtful rather than surprised. Finally he lowered his eyes, licked the paper and finished rolling the cigarette. With a grave, concentrated expression, eyes on the floor, he searched the pockets of his suit for a lighter. He finally found one in the outside pocket of his jacket, lit the cigarette and thoughtfully blew the smoke in a thin curl towards the ceiling.

'Of course I have no idea what you're talking about,' he said in a relaxed tone, almost as if he were amusing himself a little, at my expense, 'but do by all means go on.'

'I picture it like this…' I put my hands in my trouser pockets and began strolling round the studio. I kept stopping in front of the picture of the sleeping Marieke. It did indeed give off an aura of deep peace.

'You were in The Hague and, as usual when you are travelling or staying somewhere abroad, you rang home every evening to say good night, "I love you", and so on. After your wife told you several evenings running that Marieke wasn't there at the minute, was with a friend, at a Greenpeace meeting or whatever, after a while you began wondering what it was all about. And I imagine that the concern your wife couldn't quite keep out of her voice reinforced your fears. At some point you decided to go to Frankfurt in secret and see what was going on.'

'Why wouldn't I trust my wife?' he suddenly asked. 'Why would I travel in secret?' His tone of voice was entirely neutral, as if his interest in the whole thing was of a purely theoretical nature.

'Your wife was my client. In case you haven't worked it all out yet, I was the one who brought your daughter home. And at least — I don't want to offend you or your family: your wife would certainly arouse many reactions in people, but I doubt whether unconditional trust is among them.'

His upper lips twisted slightly into a smile that I found hard to interpret. Was it angry? Bitter? Amused? Or after at least sixteen years of living with her, simply tired?

'I assume there's a night train from The Hague or Amsterdam to Frankfurt, or else you came by car?'

He did not reply, just smoked and looked at me.

'Well, so once you were here you slipped into the house, probably while I was sitting with your wife in the living room. I don't know how all the rooms and back entrances connect up, but you must have had some way of listening to what we were saying. And then you heard Abakay's name and address, and you set out to save your daughter.'

I stopped in front of him. He looked at me inquiringly.

'May I roll myself a cigarette too?'

'Be my guest.' He offered me the pouch of tobacco.

I sat down on a chair covered with dried splotches of paint and helped myself to a suitable amount of tobacco.

'And I assume you rang Abakay's doorbell, but no one opened the door. Then you sat waiting in the café beside the door to the apartment building. And you ordered the dish of the day, not because you were hungry, but because by then it had occurred to you that if you were visiting someone like Abakay it would be as well to have a weapon with you.'

I licked the cigarette paper, rolled up the cigarette, and tore off the tobacco fibres hanging out of the ends.

'The waiter remembers you.'

I thought briefly of the young white man with frizzy hair who couldn't imagine a black man with racist feelings strong enough to make him attack his Turkish neighbour. *Okay, yes, there was a skewer missing at lunchtime, but I can't imagine it was your racist neighbour who nicked it.* And who hadn't dared to mention a black man's skin colour. Probably because he was afraid of bowing to racist clichés. Better not mention skin colour at all. Maybe it was the unconscious anger of many good, tolerant white people: Why the hell are we always being made to beat about the bush like this? Why can't you all be white like everyone else, and then there'd be no problem with the damn description?

'A light?' asked Hasselbaink, offering me his lighter.

'Thanks, not yet.' I was holding the cigarette between thumb and forefinger as I used to when I still smoked, and examined it for a moment in silence. 'And then you rang Abakay's bell again, and this time someone opened the door. But it was the wrong man standing in the doorway. A large, fat, bare-chested drunk, and maybe Marieke was even shouting for help in the background.'

I paused. For a moment the only sound was the crackle of Hasselbaink's burning tobacco.

'No, I don't have any children, but I can well imagine that in such a situation they are all that matters. Perhaps at first all you wanted was to get into the apartment, and Rönnthaler was in your way. Or perhaps you stabbed him at once, because the circumstances were only too clear.'

Once again I paused, and looked at the lighter in

Hasselbaink's hand. This time he didn't offer it, and I didn't want to ask.

'And then you heard me coming upstairs. Well, and so – you might say – Abakay survived.'

'But not for very long,' retorted Hasselbaink, surprisingly fast.

I cleared my throat. 'No, but that's another story. He was shot in connection with his drug dealing.'

'My wife tells the story rather differently.'

'Does she?'

'Listen,' said Hasselbaink, putting out the remains of his cigarette in the lid of a paint pot that was lying around. 'Your story, so far as the end of it goes, is pure nonsense. I didn't kill anyone, I never sat outside Abakay's apartment, and I'd like to see the white waiter who can prove convincingly that he served one coloured man rather than another in all the hustle and bustle of a café at midday…'

He smiled at me, relaxed. I thought of the waiter's description of Hasselbaink. *Age…sort of around fifty, comfortable clothes – like a professor or a nice teacher.* I was sure that Hasselbaink didn't usually go around in a bright yellow suit and no shirt. And if he got his hair under control, maybe wore a pair of reading glasses…

'All the same, there are a few details that can probably be checked, and you might make some difficulty for me with those. I really did travel by train to Frankfurt that day, because I was worried about my daughter. And I slipped into the house on the quiet, because I didn't want to alarm anyone with my surprise visit. And yes, when I heard talking in the living room I did eavesdrop on you. I don't know, but it's possible that our housekeeper, that old witch, saw me.'

He was still speaking in a calm, objective tone – too calm, too objective for my liking and for the situation, and I began to wonder what he had up his sleeve.

'But when I realised that my wife was in the process of

187

engaging a private detective to bring Marieke home, I simply sat in my studio and waited. If you want to know exactly what I thought: you made a very competent and trustworthy impression on me. I was sure you would soon be back with Marieke, and so you were. I was overjoyed when I heard you come in with her.'

'Thank you.'

'And that evening I boarded the train again and went back to the Hague.'

'Without showing yourself to either your wife or your daughter? Didn't you at least want to give them a hug?'

'Of course. But I knew it was important to both Valerie and Marieke that I didn't know they were in touch with Abakay again. I don't know how much my wife has told you, but Abakay came to supper with us one evening – an extremely unpleasant encounter.'

Once again I looked at the cigarette between my fingers. 'What do you really want to tell me, Herr Hasselbaink?'

'I want to tell you that a few days ago my wife did tell me about Abakay and you – without mentioning your name or even saying that you were a private detective. But she said she had found someone who would make sure that Abakay left us all alone, particularly Marieke, once and for all.'

He took his tobacco pouch and began rolling himself the next cigarette. His hands were perfectly steady: the hands of a painter.

'Well, my wife – as you said yourself – can arouse a number of reactions in people. At any rate, it is not entirely unimaginable that she could find a man – for suitable payment, of course – to do something for her, even something criminal. And now, I think, we both have a suspicion, totally unproven and undoubtedly false, but concrete enough to make a great deal of trouble for the other if we were to go to the police with it.'

He licked the paper, rolled up the cigarette and put it

between his lips. Then he looked up and scrutinised me attentively. 'You understand what I mean?'

I nodded.

'Good.' He lit the cigarette. After he had drawn on it twice, he said, 'You were planning to go to the police, weren't you? Otherwise you wouldn't be here.'

Suddenly I knew why he was so calm; he didn't regret anything, on the contrary. He considered the murder of the man who had been about to rape his daughter entirely justified. I assumed that even if it hadn't been possible for him to blackmail me, his hands wouldn't have trembled. And he would have gone to prison without a second thought, for saving his daughter from Rönnthaler.

I thought about his question as my fingers played with the unlit cigarette. Finally I said, 'Whether you believe it or not, I've no idea. I came here mainly out of curiosity and probably a kind of professional honour as well. I'm a private detective and I like to solve my cases.'

He smoked and thought. 'You mean in the same way as I finish painting pictures, although I know I shall neither sell them nor give them away?'

'Perhaps. I'm not an artist.'

'A light?' He offered me the lighter again.

'No, thanks. I'll be going now.' I stood up. 'I have one more request: please make it clear to your wife that she must not pass on her absurd theory about Abakay's death to anyone.'

Hasselbaink also stood up and moved his cigarette from his right to his left hand. 'You can rely on me for that.' He offered me his right hand, and I shook it. He had a firm, pleasant grasp.

'And many thanks,' he said, 'for bringing Marieke back.'

'Take care of her.'

'I'll do my best.'

I let go of his hand and nodded to him. Then I turned, left the studio, passed the laundry room and climbed the stairs to the entrance hall. The clink of crockery came from the kitchen. I left the house, went through the front garden and out into the street. As always, it was very quiet in the diplomats' district, with a smell of new-mown grass. My eyes went briefly to the bushes, but the statue had disappeared. Farther away in the garden, I thought I saw something red under a tree. Suddenly I knew what Valerie de Chavannes's stooped, care-worn stance and her empty eyes from earlier had reminded me of: whores waiting for a fix.

When I reached my bicycle I noticed that I was still holding the cigarette. I threw it into the gutter, unlocked the bike and rode away.

Without thinking about it, I cycled through the starlit night in the direction of the railway station district. I simply wanted to feel the pedals under my feet and the cool air in my face. Suddenly I saw the brightly lit ads for brothels and striptease clubs coming towards me, and I cycled on to a small, grubby dive that I knew had an old nineties jukebox.

I locked my bike and entered the gloomy room, which smelled of beer and unwashed bodies. Three old drunks sat at the bar in silence, looking up briefly when I joined them.

'A large beer,' I said to the landlord, who had greeted me with a wink. Then I went over to the jukebox, looked through the titles and found what I wanted. Soon afterwards the bar was full of the sound of Whitney Houston's 'Greatest Love of All'.

The drunks looked up in surprise. One of them grinned at me when I went back to the counter. After a while the man next to him began rocking his head dreamily in time to the music.

After my second beer I paid, wished everyone 'a good rest of the night' and left the bar feeling better.

At home I ate an apple, watched the nightly news and waited for Deborah to come home.

Chapter 17

Three weeks later Deborah and I were sitting over a late Sunday breakfast in the kitchen at the farmhouse table, which was laid with Deborah's homemade fruit muesli, soft-boiled eggs prepared by me, fresh country bread, salted butter and a pot of Assam tea. We had been up late the evening before, eating and drinking in the wine bar with Slibulsky, Lara and Deborah's sister long after it had closed, and now I felt more like a beer and some rollmops as a hangover cure than the hand-picked organic tea. But I couldn't do that to Deborah. Sunday breakfast in our West End world, which was fragrant with fresh apples and mangoes this morning, was sacred to her.

While Deborah disappeared for a moment I leafed through the new number of the *Wochenecho*. In the cultural section I looked at the list of best-selling books, and found *Journey to the End of Days* at number four. I couldn't help smiling, and I was genuinely pleased for Rashid. For five days of captivity and praying, I thought it was his just reward.

Deborah came back with two wine glasses, opened the fridge door and took out a bottle of champagne.

'Hello? I thought Sunday was our alcohol-free day?'

Deborah smiled mischievously, and her cheeks were glowing, although we hadn't touched a drop yet. 'There's something to celebrate!'

She put the glasses on the table and untwisted the wire round the cork.

'Sweetheart, you look as if you'd seen Father Christmas, the Easter bunny and a few angels all at once.'

She said nothing, just poured the champagne and raised hers aloft. I raised mine as well and asked, 'Can you tell me what we're drinking to?'

Her eyes were bright, and her voice shook slightly. 'I'm pregnant!'

My mouth dropped open, and then I said, 'Who'd have thought it!' Next moment I broke into a grin, and it just slipped off the tip of my tongue: 'And who's the father?'

Deborah's glass crashed into the wall above my head, and splinters of glass and champagne dripped on my head and shoulders. I shook myself before standing up and taking Deborah in my arms. She didn't return my embrace, but stood as stiff as a piece of wood, put her head back and looked at me fiercely.

'The father's my only remaining customer,' she said at last. 'Some shitty little Turk.'

'Little isn't right,' I objected. 'It's a cliché.'

And then at last she let me kiss her.